I0657340

Edward M Taylor

George Washington, the Ideal Patriot

Edward M Taylor

George Washington, the Ideal Patriot

ISBN/EAN: 9783744790307

Printed in Europe, USA, Canada, Australia, Japan

Cover: Foto ©Raphael Reischuk / pixelio.de

More available books at **www.hansebooks.com**

GEORGE WASHINGTON,

The Ideal Patriot.

BY

REV. EDWARD M. TAYLOR, D. D.

WITH INTRODUCTION BY
EDWARD EVERETT HALE, D. D.

CINCINNATI: CURTS & JENNINGS.
NEW YORK: EATON & MAINS.
1897.

INTRODUCTION.

BOSTON, MASS., *May 31, 1897.*

I AM most glad that my friends of the Epworth League propose to study with some care the life and character of Washington, and have so good a chance to do so.

No American boy or girl, man or woman, is equipped for life, who has not a fair acquaintance with the man Washington.

Do not make of him an idol, but think of him as a man.

NEDWARD EVERETT HALE.

3

FOREWORD.

THERE are nearly five hundred Biographies of George Washington written; they are published in almost every modern language. The story of his life has also been set in the classic forms of the Greek and Latin tongues.

His portraits adorn our Legislative Halls, and hang upon the walls of our public schools and libraries.

More than two hundred places in the United States of America bear his name. The facts of his life have all been gathered, and woven by genius into enduring forms.

Why write another book about Washington? The answer lies close at hand. Because the people do not know George Washington.

His noble, human life is not so much "first in the hearts of his.countrymen" as one might suppose.

The only right this book has to existence, is the sincere desire on the part of the author to enlist the interest of the rising generation in a thoughtful study of the *character* of George Washington.

"I am a man; I consider none of the incidents which befall my fellow-creatures to be matters of unconcern to me." These words of the Roman poet, Terence, fittingly describe the straightforward, magnanimous, and manly character of George Washington. Circumstances decreed that he should learn the lessons of life from men, rather than books. His early training was of such a nature as to put him in the closest sympathy with men and affairs. In character-study he was a master. In his long and trying career as general and President, he made but one mistake in his estimate of men. Washington was deceived in Benedict Arnold.

No man in the history of our country has left such wealth of materials from which to draw the true picture of his life as George Washington. He began the keeping of a diary in his sixteenth year, and kept it up, with but few breaks, to the end of his life, covering a period of fifty-one years. His position laid upon him the burden of a large correspondence. He has been called "the most felicitous letter-writer of the ages." He scrupulously preserved copies of his letters during his public career. Careful students of these manuscripts truthfully declare "they are his most complete biography."

Notwithstanding these facts, the *man* Washington has been submerged in the fulsome eulogies of the *hero* Washington. This practical man of affairs, in whose moral and intellectual make-up there was no moonshine, has been placed upon the lonely height of flawless greatness, far above the contemplation of the common tide of humanity. The satiric temperament finds in this picture of Washington abundant materials for work; while to ordinary mortals it reveals Washington as a character

"Too bright and good
For human nature's daily food."

It must be said in this connection that of late an earnest effort is being put forth to present Washington in his true character as a man. Dr. Edward Everett Hale * and Mr. Paul Leicester Ford †
have performed a worthy and lasting service for posterity in the careful studies they have made of the Washington manuscripts, presenting the results in such a manner that the greatest American is permitted to speak for himself.

An English artist was commissioned to paint the portrait of one of the Georges when he was the occupant of the British throne. In the finished picture the king was so profusely surrounded by sun-

---

* " George Washington Studied Anew."
† " The True George Washington."

flowers and tulips that very little of the
royal personage could be seen by the ob-
server. In some such fashion the character of the *man* George Washington has
been obscured by those who have sought
to do him honor by their services. We
have the "traditional Washington," the
"idealized Washington," the "poetic
Washington;" and the pious myth-mak-
ers, headed by the Rev. Mason Weems,
Washington's first biographer, have even
dared to starch and stiffen this plain, hon-
est Virginia planter and statesman with
their priggish man-millinery, until among
certain classes his name awakens no enthusiasm, but rather calls forth the cheap
jests so common in the "funny column"
of our newspapers.

The "cherry-tree" myth has possessed
such remarkable vitality that even to-day
it is a favorite proof-text quoted to children when the natural heart is disposed
to let truth live on debatable ground, and
our enterprising confectioners ornament

their bon-bon boxes with embossed images of that mythical "little hatchet," as a guarantee for pure candy within. Little wonder that in our childhood we found it difficult to like this juvenile Virginia prig as he was represented to us in his faultless, moral make-up. Our sympathies go out toward the precocious little girl who, when taken to task by her mother for telling an untruth, after receiving the information that "no liars ever go to heaven, George Washington never told a lie," made this deliberate answer: "Mamma, how lonesome it must be in heaven with only God and George Washington!"

From another point of view, Washington has been shut off from the sympathies of the common people. This wrong has also been done in the house of his friends. The grandiloquent eulogies of Fourth of July orations, and the overstrained rhetoric of many of his early biographers, have placed him upon the

pedestal of a demigod. Some one has
said that "four generations of statesmen
have enshrouded him in mummy clothes."
It is very easy to have our sense of
brotherhood blunted, and our feeling of
companionship obliterated, when we are
forced to look at a human being through
this cloudy, rhetorical wrappage. The
real George Washington is but dimly seen
standing in the background obscured by
shadows.

There is a legend among the New
York Indians, setting forth in dramatic
form this idea of the traditional Washington. He alone of all white men, they say,
has been admitted to the Indian heaven.
He lives in a great palace built like a fort.
All the Indians as they go to heaven pass
by, and Washington himself is in his uniform, a sword at his side, walking to and
fro. They bow reverently with great hu-
mility. He returns the salute, but says
nothing. He is too much lifted up to
speak.

By such methods has the "Father of his Country" been treated through the well-meaning intentions of his friends, that practical, serious men now write: "Washington is likely to become a mere jest;" "George Washington is now only a steel-engraving." In this year of grace, 1897, the governor of one of our great States was politely requested to furnish a sentiment on Washington's birthday. In answer to that request, he deliberately wrote these words: "We 're living at the end of the nineteenth century, and we are too busy to write sentiments about men who have been dead a hundred years." It will be a sorry day for America when the leaders in national affairs have come to the point of regarding George Washington as a "back number."

> " As stands the pyramid a mystery,
> Cleaving wedge-like the misty realm of time,
> And hides within its depth the unknown king
> 'T was built to memorize,—so common fame
> Covers with cloudy fiction all the *real man,*
> And leaves a shadow to the worshiper."

In an atmosphere composed of such trifling and traditional ingredients many of us received our first impressions of George Washington, "the noblest figure standing in the forefront of our Nation's history." The words of our latest historian, Mr. McMaster, are worthy of our attention at this point: "General Washington is known to us, and President Washington; but George Washington is an unknown man."

In the study I have been commissioned to make of this imperial man, the principal end to be attained is to tell the story of Washington's life so that the reader may be in constant touch with him as a man. To lay bare the fact, if possible, that all that General Washington and President Washington did for our country came out of the character of George Washington *the man.* The significance of his life is, in a measure, lost to posterity if we ignore the truth that what Washington did for his country is a like possibility for every

American citizen, according to the measure of the stewardship committed to his
care.

All that George Washington ever became was brought about through the discipline and development of his better self.
He was a great master of affairs, but his
greatest victory was the mastery he obtained over himself. Out of such discipline came the clear-headed, clean-
hearted man, the successful planter, the
genial neighbor, the devoted husband, the
ideal patriot, the brave soldier, and the
incorruptible statesman. We must remember that when Washington received
his commission as commander-in-chief of
the Continental army he was forty-three
years of age. In the stirring scenes of the
Revolution he seems to have sprung suddenly into world-wide notoriety, like Mi-
nerva into "full-orbed life from the head
of Jupiter." But behind this general on
horseback were the formative periods and
processes of his manhood. All the ele-

ments entering into that character of imperial leadership and organizing skill had hardened into moral muscle and intellectual fiber before he received his commission. This work was accomplished between the years 1732 and 1775, amid scenes and surroundings of Colonial Virginia. Botanists tell us that in studying the life of a plant we should enter the zone of its natural abode. To push our investigations of its nature amid the artificial surroundings of the conservatory is to do the plant a wrong, and obtain for ourselves only partial knowledge. It is certainly a wise method in the study of men. Clothing this truth in another form, we might say, as the water of certain rivers derives its coloring matter from the rocks and soils through which it percolates far away in the mountain gorges, so the *man* Washington assimilated certain elements found in the social, intellectual, and political life of the Old Dominion.

CONTENTS.

CHAPTER I.

PAGE.

THE OLD DOMINION, ... 17

CHAPTER II.

CAVALIER AND PURITAN, ... 28

CHAPTER III.

ANCESTRY AND BIRTH, ... 46

CHAPTER IV.

BOYHOOD AND HOME LIFE, ... 56

CHAPTER V.

SCHOOL DAYS, ... 71

CHAPTER VI.

LEAVING THE HOME NEST, ... 88

CHAPTER VII.

TROUBLE ON THE FRONTIER, ... 104

CHAPTER VIII.

UNDER FIRE, ... 121

15

CHAPTER IX.

PAGE.

MARRIAGE AND MOUNT VERNON, ... 145

CHAPTER X.

STIRRING THE EAGLE'S NEST, ... 165

CHAPTER XI.

COMMANDER-IN-CHIEF AND PRESIDENT, . . . 184

CHAPTER XII.

WASHINGTON'S VISION OF THE WEST, . . 213

CHAPTER XIII.

WORDS OF WASHINGTON, ... 230

CHAPTER XIV.

SAYINGS OF WASHINGTON, ... 261

GEORGE WASHINGTON.

CHAPTER I.

THE OLD DOMINION.

T HE social and political institutions of America, founded by English Colonists in the New World, are the joint products of two distinct centers of population—New England and the Old Dominion. Plymouth in Massachusetts, and Jamestown in Viriginia, are the two memorable spots in the Western Hemisphere, where were planted and nurtured the men and principles which have produced the American Commonwealth.

The history of New England and of her principles has been fully and ably written. Nobly has the scholarship of New England paid its debt of gratitude to the land of the Pilgrim and the Puritan. Her literary sons and daughters have produced an historic literature, in which the story of her development has been faithfully recorded from her Colonial days to the present hour. The history of the Old Dominion has been unworthily written. The one hundred and two Cavalier Colonists, who planted the Jamestown Settlement in 1607, have had scant justice from the pen of the historian. The development of this colony of Royalists into the staunch democracy of Revolutionary times is an interesting and suggestive study, and it is to be hoped that Virginia, the great historic Commonwealth of the South, which stood as the companion of Massachusetts in the Colonial, Revolutionary, and Constitutional periods of our

country's development, shall yet have her
story told by as able pens and sympathetic
hearts, as those who have done a like
service for New England.

The cause of this neglect is easily dis-
covered, when we carefully contrast the
conditions existing in those primitive
days of Virginia life with the existing
conditions in New England life. The
two Colonies were alike only in their common heritage of suffering; both were
nearly destroyed through epidemic, disaster, and massacre.

The Cavaliers were intense Royalists,
while the New Englanders were turbu-
lent yet pious Roundheads. In religion,
the Virginians were Episcopalians, and
zealous advocates of the union of Church
and State; while the New England Colonists were Congregationalists, whose
slogan was "a Church without a bishop,

and a State without a king." In social life the Cavalier was a patrician. In New England the Pilgrim was a plebeian. In Virginia the almighty dollar was the potent factor in the scheme of colonization. In New England it was religious enthusiasm and liberty of conscience.

The settlement at Jamestown was the earliest English colony on the American continent. Its roots were planted in the New World's soil thirteen years before the *Mayflower* brought the Pilgrims to Plymouth Rock. These Virginia Colonists set sail from London on December 19, 1606. The fleet consisted of three vessels, bearing the names of the *Discovery*, the *Goodspeed*, and the *Susan Content*. The entire passenger list numbered one hundred and two souls. As they moved down the Thames and arched their sails for the far-off shores of the New World, all London turned out to wish them God-speed. Special prayer services were held in the churches on their behalf, and many of the poets eulogized in song their adventurous enterprise. Here is a sample from the pen of Drayton:

> "You brave heroic minds,
>   Worthy your country's name,
>   That honor still pursue;
> Whilst loitering hinds
>   Lurk here at home with shame,
>   Go and subdue.

> "And cheerfully at sea
>   Success you still entice
> To get the pearls and gold,
>   And ours to hold
>   Virginia,
>   Earth's only paradise."

After a five-months' voyage over the Atlantic, the three ships dropped their anchors in James River, on the 13th of May, 1607. True to their Cavalier traditions, they named the port of their landing Jamestown, after King James I, the then reigning king of England.

In imagination let us bridge the chasm of time that yawns between the present hour and that far-away bright May-day of 1607. An Indian will take us in his canoe out to these vessels as they swing at their anchor-chains in the tide currents of the great river. We are permitted to go on board each vessel, and make our tour of inspection. Some interesting and suggestive revelations are in store for us. In the sailing list we find a strange classi-fication of passengers. It reads as fol-lows: "Gentlemen, carpenters, laborers, gold-refiners, jewelers, and one per-fumer." A closer analysis of the list re-veals the fact that more than one-half of the entire number are listed as "gentle-men"—that term in those times indicating a man who thought it degrading to engage in manual labor.

As we look shoreward, we see the trackless forest pressing to the very edge of tide-water, portions of which must be cleared away; a virgin soil to be broken for purposes of agriculture; wharves to be constructed, and houses to be built with timber from the stump; the endurance of hardships and deprivations peculiar to frontier life; and, hanging over all, the serious dangers from the prowling savage. Are these "gentlemen" Colonists equal to the herculean task? The outlook is full of the omens of failure.

There is another discovery to be made in relation to this Virginia Colony—a discovery which is little short of startling, in view of all it portends. There is not a woman to be found in the whole company. By all laws governing human development in any department of our world's life, this band of Colonists is doomed to failure, unless the ennobling influence of woman is brought into co-operation with their efforts. Of all men in the world, how could an Englishman hope to attain any success without the nucleus of his home life? That has been the chief secret of his invincible colonizing power. His march to victory has been secured by the fact that he carried his home with him wherever he went. Very early in the history of our race the Almighty pronounced a bachelor a failure, and hastened to relieve the situation by creating a woman as "an helpmeet" for him in the serious work of life. A discriminating writer puts the whole matter in these forceful words: "What could we expect from a hundred and two old bachelors—

a community of bachelors? It is as much
as society can do to get along with one
here and there in the community; a colony of bachelors never carried any cause
on earth to a successful conclusion, and
never will."

Events in the Colony soon began to
shape themselves according to existing
conditions; the process of disintegration
set in, and the men were rapidly taking on
the nature of savages in their treatment
of each other. Through the influence of
the beautiful Indian girl, Pocahontas, the
Colony was saved from extinction. The
lax condition of affairs became known in
England, and wise measures were suggested and carried out by men upon
whose hearts the interests of the scheme
lay heavily. Virginia must be looked
upon as *home* by the adventurers. If the
plantation were ever to become a success-

ful enterprise, the double magnet of wife and child must hold these discouraged emigrants to the arduous work of colonization. Sir Edwin Sandys, in a wise stroke of statemanship, devised a plan whereby one hundred fair daughters, with irreproachable characters, should volunteer to go out to Virginia from the Mother Country, with the distinct understanding that they were to become the wives of the struggling Colonists. The expense of their voyage and outfit was considerable, and this was to be met by those who selected them for wedlock, the price being fixed at one hundred and twenty pounds of tobacco—about eighty dollars in American money.

The scheme is apt to strike the mind of the humorist as furnishing material for a new "Comedy of Errors." To the conservative mind of to-day it is highly seasoned with the commercial view of marriage. It, however, saved the Colony of Virginia from extinction, giving it a new lease of life, and starting it upon a prosperous career.

This shipload of English "maids," as they are called by the old chronicler, arrived in Jamestown twelve years after the landing of the original Colonists. The record of the time states that within twenty-four hours after their landing the majority of these maidens had become the wives of the Colonists; the minister of the Colony, it is said, making a "snug little fortune." It is, I believe, the only day in the history of America in which the office of a parson may be said to have been tempting to the candidate in the matter of dimes and dollars.

CHAPTER II.

CAVALIER AND PURITAN.

THE statement has already been made that the history of New England has been fully written, while that of Virginia has been but partially depicted. The cause of this is easily explained by the scientific doctrine of conformity to type. It will serve our purpose to compare the manners and laws of our Colonial forefathers, as represented by these Cavalier and Puritan communities. Their social and political ideas were entirely different before they united in the general round-up to secure American Independence.

At no point in their history is the contrast greater than in their respective opinions concerning popular education.

28

In New England the school-house stood
side by side with the Church; they were
the two pillars, Jachin and Boaz, of Puritan institutions. In 1640, just twenty
years after the landing at Plymouth Rock,
the New England Colony had created a
university. In 1647 we find an established
system of education throughout her borders. A touching picture presents itself
as we look backward to those early years
of New England life, where the Pilgrims,
impoverished as to resources and ignorant of New World conditions, with
"short allowance of victual and plenty of
nothing but gospel," were forced to take
lessons in agriculture from the Indian
brave, Tisquantum, who tells them that
Indian corn, which was to be their main
dependence, "should be sown when the
leaves of the oak were as big as the ears
of a mouse." This sorely-tried and over-

taxed Colonist reveals the force of his convictions when we see him part with his last cent, paying it to his township as a school-tax; formulating his conscience into a simple yet severe law, reading as follows: "Every township, after the Lord hath increased them to the number of fifty households, shall appoint one to teach all children to read and write, and when any town shall increase to the number of a hundred families, they shall set up a common school; the masters thereof being able to instruct youth, so far as they may be fitted for the university." Here we uncover the springs of New England's literary fountains.

In the early life of the Old Dominion a different condition of affairs existed. There is little indication that the planters of Virginia had any sympathy with the cause of popular education. Few of the people thought that "becoming a mere scholar" was "a desirable education for a gentleman." The gentleman was to "become acquainted with men and things, rather than books." In 1671, when the white population of Virginia numbered forty thousand souls, the Colonial governor, Berkeley; was willing to thank God that they had "no free schools nor printing," and hoped that "we shall not have any these hundred years, for learning has brought disobedience, heresy, and sects into the world, and printing has divulged them with libels against the best government. God keep us from both!" During the first fifty years of Virginia's history there were no public schools, and at the breaking out of the Revolution, in 1775, there was scarcely any system of public education within the borders of the Colony. When the Virginia Commis-

sioners interviewed the attorney-general
of Charles II in reference to an appropriation for the cause of learning and religion in Virginia, they were answered with
an oath: "Go home and grow tobacco."
This was popular sentiment in Virginia
for more than a hundred years.

It will best serve our purpose at this
point to take into consideration the
Royalist inclinations of these Virginia
Colonists. There is no doubt that at heart
the great body of the population of Virginia were in full sympathy with the king
at the time of the English Revolution
under Cromwell. The origin of the term
"Old Dominion," by which Virginia is
known to this day, indicates that the sentiment of Virginia was decidedly on the
side of royalty in those stormy times. The
execution of Charles I was treason according to the vote of the Virginia Bur-

gesses in 1649. This vote fixed a penalty upon those who should, "by words or speeches, endeavor to insinuate any doubt, scruple, or question concerning the right of His Majesty that now is to the Colony of Virginia." The king the Virginians thus recognized was the exiled son of the beheaded Charles I, who had sought refuge on the Continent, but these Virginians recognized him as the ruler, Charles II, by "Divine right" King of England and of all other of His Majesty's dominions the moment his father's head rolled from the scaffold.

It was dangerous work thus to deal with Cromwell; for the great ruler had a strong arm, and he could reach very far—even across the Atlantic. His power he soon put into operation, and sent one of his warships to Virginia, forcing the Cavalier Colonists into tranquillity during his protectorate. The great Oliver subdued them, but he did not extinguish the flame of devotion to royalty burning in the Cavalier heart.

Sir William Berkeley, the governor of the Colony at this time, sent Colonel Richard Lee, a rich planter, to visit Charles II on the Continent, and offered him the Colony of Virginia as his kingdom, requesting that he come and set up his standard on Virginian soil. Charles did not look with favor upon the offer, but he ever afterwards held the kindness of the Virginians in grateful remembrance. Tradition says that after his restoration, he recognized the fidelity of his Virginia subjects by wearing a coat of Virginia silk on the day of his coronation. Afterwards, when coins were minted under the reign of Charles II, they bore the inscription: "England, Scotland,

Ireland, and Virginia." One of these coins is now in the possession of the Massachusetts Historical Society in Boston, and may be seen by the lover of American antiquities.

The term "Old Dominion" is said to have originated in this incident in the life of the exiled king, indicating the fact that he might have had a throne and dominion in Virginia before he was crowned King of the British Empire.

A few words descriptive of the social and political life of Virginia previous to the Revolution will close this chapter. A glance at the map of Eastern Virginia shows it to be a highly-favored land as to natural resources. Blessed with an extensive coast-line, it is also favored with that fan-like river system, made up of the Potomac, Rappahannock, York, and James Rivers. The fertile valleys and uplands lying along these river courses invited the planters to settle and develop the natural resources of the country.

It is interesting to note the way in which the seductive narcotic found in the tobacco-leaf played such an important part in the development of plantation-life in Old Virginia. About the time of the settlement of the Colony, Sir Walter Raleigh introduced the custom of tobacco-smoking among the fashionable people of England, and as early as 1610 tobacco was in general use throughout England. The rich land lying along the shores of these great rivers soon became famous for the quality and quantity of tobacco it would produce. Out of this condition the great plantation-life of Virginia was developed. During the year 1619 England imported twenty thousand pounds of Virginia tobacco. Tobacco was the medium of exchange; the planter ordered his goods from England, and paid for them in tobacco. Taxes were paid in tobacco, and so was even the salary of the minister of the gospel. A Colonial officer was appointed in every plantation to collect the parson's portion out of the "first and best tobacco." It was their way of presenting the first-fruits of their increase unto the Lord.

This ready market required a great number of laborers on the plantations to supply the increasing demand. English farmers could not be induced to leave their homes in England, and· come to America as laborers on the great plantations. They were much needed at home, and did not care to exchange a sure thing for the hardships and uncertainties of frontier life. The social condition of the poorer classes in English cities was then

very much as it is now. Every large city
was crowded with poor people, who could
not find employment. Many of these
were sent to America as servants and
laborers, the plantation owners of Virginia paying the expenses of the voyage,
and the emigrant in return binding himself to his employer for a certain number
of years.

There was much trial and difficulty
connected with this system of "indentured
servants," as it was called. The experi-
ment was not a success from the view-
point of the planter. Many of these servants were habitual idlers; others had been
criminals in the Old World, and brought
over with them nothing in the shape of
trustworthy characters. In some cases
the work of a plantation overseer was
much like that of a prison warden.

In all such moments of trial, the old-

time enemy, the devil, is found to be near
at hand with suggestions and flattering
propositions. On this occasion he sailed
up the James River on board a Dutch
man-of-war with twenty captive Negroes
from the coast of Africa. The Virginia
planters in the neighborhood thought
they saw a way out of the difficulties occasioned by the shipment of laborers from
the slums of English cities. They purchased the Negroes, and held them as
slaves in a life of perpetual bondage.

This took place in the month of August, 1619, the year before the Pilgrims
landed at Plymouth Rock. This same
year Virginia had been granted what was
substantially free government. A "General Assembly" was to be called, the members thereof being elected by the votes·of
the free men in Virginia. This legislative
body held its first meeting, July 30th, at

Jamestown. It was the first body representing free government that ever sat in
America. Thus, within one month of each
other, free government and African slavery were introduced upon the American
continent. A strange combination! Yet
from that hour it produced a storm center
in America's political life, growing darker
and darker, until it finally broke in the
terrible cyclone of our Civil War.

We have here the materials out of
which were framed the social life of Old
Virginia in her most prosperous days.
One-half of the population were *slaves*. A
step upward in the social scale, we have the
middle class, whites composed of "indentured servants," who had served out their
contracts with the great planters, and in
many cases had become small landholders, locating upon the shores of the tributaries to the great rivers above the points

of navigation, floating their produce of wheat and tobacco in flatboats down the streams to the wharves of the great planters. This class included also the hunters, pioneers, traders, merchants, and mechanics, scattered here and there throughout the country. Another step upward in the social scale, and we reach the highest point of Virginia social life, composed of professional men and the great plantation owners, modeled after the manner of the English landholder. These were the men "who owned, ruled, and guided Virginia." They had plenty of leisure, and the sporting proclivities for which Virginia gentlemen were renowned had their origin with this class.

These conditions of life were not favorable to the development of towns and cities representing centers of population, as in New England. As a result, the country became the unit of political power in Virginia, and the township, represented by the town-meeting, formed the political unit in New England.

These squire landholders, as they were called, formed the aristocracy of Virginia. They were men with a genius for government; they knew how to rule. They were not an aristocracy of idlers. The cares and labors peculiar to overseeing their great plantations kept them in touch with practical affairs, and it is not surprising to find the legislative assemblies made up of this class of men. There was little inclination among these "First Families of Virginia" to become scholars; but there was something in their habits and dispositions that made practical and thoughtful men of them, qualifying them for that leadership in public affairs for which the

Old Dominion was so renowned in the period of our Revolution.

New England produced the agitators and forced into existence popular institutions. Virginia furnished the great leaders, and formulated the methods by which popular institutions were placed upon enduring foundations. This is one of the paradoxes of history, and yet the cold facts of the record force us to the statement. Could a more hopeless seed-plot be found in which to grow the material for democratic institutions than this very Virginia, into whose early life we have been looking? And yet what happened? A hotbed of Puritan-hating Cavaliers, modeled on the plan of English aristocracy, was transformed into a revolutionary democracy. Rising above ancestral tradition, selfish pride, and prejudice, they proved themselves able to discard their past, and rise with an intense yet well-balanced devotion to the vision of justice as presented in the equal rights of all men. These contradictions, like the struggling and conflicting influences of breeze and rudder, contended against each other only to secure the sure progress of the ship. It was a Virginian, Patrick Henry, whose fiery eloquence kindled the flames of the Revolution, whose words, "Give me liberty, or give me death," were emblazoned upon the battle-flags of Colonial troops, and carried as their slogan into the contest. It was Thomas Jefferson, of Virginia, called the "Apostle of Democracy," who penned our sacred document, the Declaration of Independence. James Madison, a Virginian, drafted the Constitution of the United States. It was Virginia who gave us her

imperial son, George Washington, at the
call of John Adams, to lead the destinies
of the Continental armies from the siege
of Boston to the surrender of Cornwallis
at Yorktown.

> "Virginia gave us this imperial man,
>   Cast in the massive mold
>   Of those high-statured ages old,
> Which into grander forms our mortal metal
>   ran ;
> She gave us this unblemished gentleman,—
>   What shall we give her back but love and
>   praise?"   —*Lowell.*

CHAPTER III.

ANCESTRY AND BIRTH.

IT is a coincidence worthy of note, that George Washington, the Father of his Country, and Abraham Lincoln, the Savior of his Country, were alike indifferent to ancestral connections. "My early history," said Lincoln, "is perfectly characterized by a single line of Gray's Elegy: 'The short and simple annals of the poor.'" After Washington had become famous, when the eyes of the world were upon him, and his family history was under investigation, he wrote to one who was interested in his pedigree: "It is of very little moment; a subject to which, I confess, I have paid very little attention."

They were both men of such sterling char-

46

acter, taking such practical views of life, that they regarded the development of personal virtues of more consequence than an inherited pedigree. Tennyson's lines are suitable in their application to each of these choice products of American manhood:

> "Howe'er it be, it seems to me,
> 'T is only noble to be good;
> Kind hearts are more than coronets,
> And simple faith than Norman blood."

In looking over Washington's letters pertaining to family matters, it would seem that he had sufficient care and expense in looking after the children of his brothers and sisters to excuse him from any investigations along the line of his ancestors. "God left him childless, that he might be the father of his country," is a very beautiful poetic conception; but Washington turned his childless condition into innumerable fatherly benefits among the more prolific households of his brothers and his sister Betty. The elements of thrift, honesty, and greatness, were unsparingly bestowed upon George Washington; but among his own brothers, and in many cases in their children, there was very little capacity for doing anything but making care and trouble for their illustrious relative.

His favorite brother, John, who was his junior by four years, must here be mentioned as an exception. Washington describes him as "the intimate companion of my youth, and the friend of my ripened age."

His brother Samuel, two years his junior, was a man of expensive habits and prodigal with his money—a tendency he carried into his matrimonial affairs, having been married five times. Of him,

Washington wrote to another brother: "In God's name, how did my brother Samuel get himself so enormously in debt?"

Yet George Washington had whereof to boast in the line of his ancestry. The Washington family appears with honorable mention on the pages of English history in the early days of the civil war, where the Washingtons of Sulgrave are represented as strong supporters of the king. One, Sir Henry by name, "fought gallantly under Rupert at the storming of Bristol, in 1643," and "in 1646 defended Worcester against Fairfax." The Washington family in England were a race of thrifty people, owning lands, holding positions as magistrates, possessing the qualities of good soldiers, with a dominating tendency to make good marriages.

The family first made its appearance

4

in Virginia in 1658, when two brothers, John and Lawrence Washington, bought lands at Bridges Creek, in Westmoreland County. This John Washington was the first paternal ancestor of George Washington on the American continent, and in the line of family ascent stands related to our Washington as great-grandfather. Soon after his arrival in America, his English wife and two children died. Shortly after this bereavement, he married a second time, selecting as his companion a woman of good family by the name of Anne Pope, by whom he had three children—Lawrence, John, and Anne. Judging from the positions he held in the Colony, he was a man of character and influence, having been elected to the House of Burgesses in 1667, just ten years after his arrival in the Colony. Eight years later

we find him holding the office of colonel
in the Virginia militia.

At his death, according to the English
law, whereby the right of inheritance be-
longs to the eldest son, Lawrence Washington became the head of the family.
Lawrence married Mildred Warner, a
woman from one of the "gentry families"
of Virginia. This union was blessed with
three children—John, Augustine, and
Mildred Washington.

This second son, Augustine, was the
father of George Washington. Early in
life he was sent to England, and received
his education at Appleby school. During
his early manhood he followed the sea for
a time, and then settled down on the Virginia plantation as an industrious and
prosperous planter, raising "corn, horned
beasts, swine, and tobacco." At twenty-

one years of age he was first married to Jane Butler, by whom he had three sons and a daughter—Butler, Lawrence, Augustine, and Jane—Butler and Jane dying in childhood. Fifteen months after the death of his first wife, Augustine Washington, the father, was married a second time to Mary Ball, a woman of striking beauty, and one of the belles of the neighborhood. She bore him four sons and two daughters—George, Elizabeth (called Betty), Samuel, John Augustine, Charles, and Mildred. In the quaint language of the time, Augustine Washington describes these marriages in his will as "several ventures."

George, the first-born of this second marriage, came into this world Saturday, February 22, 1732. At the time of his birth, his father was thirty-eight years old, his mother was twenty-eight. He was the fifth child of ten children by his father, and the first child of six children borne by his mother. The old Family Bible bears this record concerning this fate-marked babe: "George Washington, son of Augustine and Mary, his wife, was born ye eleventh day of February, 1731½,* about ten in the morning, and was baptized the 3d of April following." The house in which the family lived at this time stood near the Potomac River, at a place called Bridges Creek, in Washington Parish, Westmoreland County. It had been the home of the Washingtons

---

* "Double dating of the year, as is done here, was an old custom observed between January 1st and the 25th of March. For all other portions of the year a single date was used. Although January 1st had been generally accepted as the beginning of the historical year in Christian countries, yet March 25th was held by some as the beginning of the civil or legal year. The Gregorian Chronology, or *new style*, had not, at the time of Washington's birth, been adopted by England, and, indeed, was not until September 2, 1752."

By the adoption of Pope Gregory's Calendar, eleven days were added to the reckoning, thus bringing Washington's birthday on the date of February 22d, the day now observed.

since the landing of the first ancestor in
1657. The old house has been frequently
described. Its counterpart may be seen
to-day in certain parts of Old Virginia
and in rural New England. It was a
plain, wooden farm-house, with four
rooms on the ground floor; above these
was an attic story, a long roof sloping
nearly to the ground on the rear side;
with great brick chimneys at each end,
affording abundant space for the large,
open fireplaces within. Three years after
Washington was born, the house was
burned to the ground. Not a trace of the
old house is in existence to-day, and the
only way of identifying the spot where
the great leader of Democratic America
was born, is by a stone slab, weather-
beaten and overgrown with briers, rest-
ing upon a foundation of bricks taken

from the ruins of the old chimneys. The
little monument bears this inscription:

HERE,

The 11th of Febuary, 1732, (old style,)

GEORGE WASHINGTON

WAS BORN.

"Honored and loved—the patriot and the sage—
Born for thine own and every coming age;
Thy country's champion, Freedom's chosen son,
We hail thy birthday—glorious Washington."
—*S. F. Smith, D. D.,*
(Author of "My Country, 't is of Thee.")

CHAPTER IV.

BOYHOOD AND HOME LIFE.

THE burning of the house on Bridges Creek left the family without a home. Augustine Washington having business interests in some iron-works in another part of the Colony, and wishing to bring up his children with other surroundings than those furnished by the lonely neighborhood of Bridges Creek, decided to rebuild his home in another locality. He was the owner of an estate in Stafford County, on the east side of the Rappahannock River, and to this estate he removed his family, locating at a point on the river opposite the village of Fredericksburg. The second house in which the family lived is not now in existence,

56

but an accurate picture was made of it before it was destroyed. It was very much after the style of the old house at Bridges Creek. It stood on the slope of a gradually rising hill, with a stretch of meadow-land between it and the Rappahannock, in full view of Fredericksburg, just across the river. This home was called "Pine Grove" by the Washington family, but in the neighborhood it was known as "Ferry Farm."

In this picturesque spot George Washington spent his childhood, surrounded by such wholesome and vigorous life as the well-kept plantation and grandly-flowing river presented. It must have been a very happy childhood. Here were developed that intense love for athletic sports and the delight in outdoor life for which Washington showed such passionate fondness through all the years of his mature manhood. Here the great mother, Nature, took the boy into her arms, and nursed him into loving fellowship with her mighty forests, fruitful fields, and majestic rivers.

Mr. B. J. Lossing, in "The Home of Washington," gives us a glance into the childhood period of Washington's life at this time. Among his early boy companions was Richard Henry Lee, a member of one of the famous families of Virginia. In after years they had much to do with each other, when serious matters of the Revolution pressed upon them. Here is a sample of their first letter-writing at nine years of age:

"Richard Henry Lee to George Washington:

"Pa brought me two pretty books full of pictures he got them in Alexandria they have pictures of dogs and cats and tigers and elefants and ever so many pretty things cousin bids me send you one of them it has a picture of an elefant and a little Indian boy on his back like uncle jo's sam pa says if I learn my tasks good he will let uncle jo bring me to see you will you ask your ma to let you come to see me.   RICHARD HENRY LEE."

"George Washington to Richard Henry Lee:

"DEAR DICKEY I thank you very much for the pretty picture-book you gave me. Sam asked me to show him the pictures and I showed him all the pictures in it; and I read to him how the tame elephant took care of the master's little boy, and put him on his back and would not let any body touch his master's little son. I can read three or four pages sometimes without missing a word. Ma says I may go to see you, and stay all day with you next week if it be not rainy. She says I may ride my pony Hero if Uncle Ben will go with me and lead Hero. I have a little piece of poetry about the picture book you gave me, but I must n't tell you who wrote the poetry.

"'G. W.'s compliments to R. H. L.
And likes his book full well,
Henceforth will count him his friend,
And hopes many happy days he may spend.'
"Your good friend,
• "GEORGE WASHINGTON.

"I am going to get a whip top soon, and you may see and whip it."

Washington has the general reputation of being a "nonconformist in the use of the king's English." He certainly does well in this letter for a boy of nine years. If he wrote the poetry with which he closes the letter, posterity has occasion to rejoice that the Muse deserted him very early in life.

A dark shadow now falls across the threshold of this prosperous and happy home. The family had lived nine years in the new home on the Rappahannock when Augustine Washington was taken sick as the result of exposure in a severe rainstorm, and on the 12th day of April, 1743, he died, being forty-nine years of age. His body was taken to Bridges Creek, and placed in the family tomb.

George Washington was eleven years old at the time of his father's death. The boy had early shown signs of future promise, and the father dearly loved the lad, taking him into a close companionship

with himself; doing that which sturdy,
energetic business men so seldom find
congenial—making a chum out of his
boy.

After the death of Augustine Washington the family numbered eight souls—
Lawrence and Augustine, Jr., the two
sons of the former marriage; the widowed
mother; George, the first-born of the
second marriage, and four younger children. The estate of the father at the time
of his death consisted of five thousand
acres of land lying in four counties, several town lots in Fredericksburg, and one-
twelfth of the shares in the Principio Iron
Company. To Lawrence, the eldest son,
fell the lion's share—two thousand five
hundred acres of land near Hunting
Creek, now Mount Vernon; also other
lands and the iron-works shares. To Augustine, the rich lands in Westmoreland

County, the first home of the Washington family in America. To George he willed the plantation and mansion on the Rappahannock, where the family were living at the time of his death. To the wife and younger children were given the residue of the estate. Augustine Washington's confidence in the ability and prudence of his wife is indicated by a clause in his will, where he directs that all the proceeds of the property given to the minor children should be administered by her until they became of age. George Washington's tender regard for the comfort of his mother finds generous expression in that he never claimed from her the part of the estate left to him by his father.

In many of the efforts to describe the character of "Mary, the mother of Washington," much use has been made of sentimental imagination plus the process of going beyond the truth. She has been represented as a prodigy of motherhood, as a personality fabulous in womanly resources. Other delineators of her character swing to the opposite extreme, proceeding upon the principle of human frailty, that milk spilled from one side of the pan must also be spilled from the other side in the act of readjustment. According to this estimate of Mother Washington, she possessed some of the characteristics of a common scold. Her intense solicitude for her son George has been described as "fond and unthinking." She lived to be eighty-three years of age, her death preceding that of her son by ten years. In the last years of her life she was a great sufferer from a cancer. Under the pressure of this disease and the weight of years, a querulous discontent, so frequently the heritage of old age grew upon her. This tendency to petulance, growing out of these abnormal conditions, has been worked in some quarters into the belief that it was a constituent element of her character when left as a healthy, sagacious, young widow in charge of a large plantation with five young children under her care.

In each of these representations a wrong is done to the memory of Mary Washington. Her real character is sufficiently strong and noble to stand alone without the aid of fulsome eulogy, and posterity will tolerate no attempt to minimize her influence upon the character of her son by dragging into the light certain frailties so common to humanity "when age steals on."

Sir Matthew Hale's "Contemplations Moral and Divine" was Mary Washington's hand-book of duty. This precious volume, bearing his mother's name, written by her own hand, Washington preserved with filial care till the day of his death. It may still be seen in the archives of Mount Vernon. If she had performed for him no other service than that of teaching him to venerate the contents of this book, she would have done enough to lay the foundations of his noble character. Here is the closing paragraph of a selection from these Contemplations, used by Mary Washington as a memory lesson for her children: "When Thy honor or the good of my country was concerned, I then thought it was a seasonable time to lay out my reputation for the advantage of either, and to act with it, and by it, and upon it, to the highest, in the use of all lawful means, and upon such an occasion, the counsel of Mordecai to Esther was my encouragement: *'Who knoweth*

*whether God hath not given thee this repu-
tation and esteem for such a time as this.'* "
One feels as if he were in the council
chambers of the Almighty as he reads
these words, and then thinks of Washington during the struggle for liberty.

Few facts are known concerning the
life of Mary Washington after the death
of her husband. Combining these with
the sidelights that fall across the pathway
of her widowhood, we discover a woman-
hood intensely human. Her character is
revealed as being neither above nor be-
neath that of hundreds of other American mothers, who have been called to pass
through similar experiences.

Returning to her home from the funeral of her husband, she is confronted by
the serious problems of administering her
husband's estate, caring for and training
five fatherless children. She was a sensi-

ble, high-minded woman, with much of
the old Roman matron in her make-up,
and having small store of polite accom-
plishments. To a woman of conscience,
life is a terribly serious affair from such
a point of view.

To the tasks of administering her business matters and training her children for
their future destiny, this mother, now
thirty-seven years of age, addresses herself. She took up with earnest heart and
helping hands the responsibilities before
her, setting' herself with steadfast purpose to hear and obey the calls of duty.

To a woman of Madam Washington's
temperament there belonged a settled
conviction that a home must do something more for a boy than to give him
shelter by night and food by day, with the
opportunity of *growing up* to man's es-

tate.   She was a contender for *home training:*

She very early recognized in her shy, grave, full-blooded first-born a dynamo of tremedous energy. She had given him much of her own strong nature, and therefore knew his possibilities under the sway of strong passion. Virginia at this time had her share of young rakes, recruited from the first families, and even her boy might be tempted beyond the point of endurance. Madam Washington set herself the task of avoiding such disaster by administering the affairs of her home according to strict discipline. She "trained the children in manners and morals, in ideas and in faith, day and night, morning and evening." Her word was law. Generally it was tenderly administered; but if necessity required it, sterner meth-

ods were adopted, from which there was
no appeal.

Lawrence Washington, of Chotank—a
cousin of George Washington—writes
these words concerning Mary Washington and her family life: "I was often here
[at Pine Grove] with George, his play-
mate, schoolmate, and young man's companion. Of the mother, I was more afraid
than of my own parents. She awed me
in the midst of her kindness; and even
now, when time has whitened my locks
and I am the grandfather of a second
generation, I could not behold that majestic woman without feelings it is impossible to describe."

No doubt this would be called heroic
treatment in the light of modern sentiment; but it put iron into the blood, and
taught with no uncertain sound the two
great principles of modern civilization,

self-restraint and obedience to law.   In after years, when the fame of George Washington was world-wide, he often repeated these words of tribute to his mother's care: "All that I am, I owe to my mother."

CHAPTER V.

SCHOOL-DAYS.

W HILE the public-school system received little sympathy and less
support in the early days of Virginia life, we are not to infer that there
were no educated men in Virginia. The
"first families," very early in the history of
the Colony, sent their sons to English uni-
versities. At the period of Washington's
boyhood, Virginia was well supplied with
men who had received their degrees from
Oxford and Edinburgh. There was a
students' club in the University of Edinburgh, whose membership conditions required one "to have been born in Virginia."

George Washington's father had re-

ceived his education at Appleby School
in England, and, true to his English in-
stincts, he sent Lawrence and Augustine,
the two sons by his first marriage, to the
Mother Country to complete their education. Shortly before the father's death
Lawrence returned from England, an educated and finished gentleman, according
to the standards of that day. He was a
man of noble, generous character, the senior of his half-brother George by fourteen
years, and from the hour of his father's
death he took his little step-brother upon
his heart, loving him with a double affection, and aiding him in every possible
way. "Big brother Lawrence was the
hero of George's youth."

Had Augustine Washington lived,
doubtless George would have shared with
his older half-brothers the advantages of
a thorough scholastic training. What ef-

fect an English university education might
have wrought on the future life and service of George Washington, no one has the
right to say. But this may be said, backed
by the sober facts of experience, three
times in the early life of Washington did
the genius of American destiny shut her
iron door against him, forbidding him to
come into any closer relations with English official life than those of a colonel of
Virginia Militia.

When the family removed from their
home at Bridges Creek to "Pine Grove"
on the Rappahannock, George was sent
to the old·"Field School," taught by a
Mr. Hobly, pedagogue, and sexton of the
parish. Tradition says this schoolmaster
carried about with him more English conceit than any man in three parishes. Here
our hero, a strong, healthy country boy,
learned the alphabet and the first prin-

ciples of writing. Soon after his father's death, when just entering his twelfth year, he was sent back to Bridges Creek, the home of his half-brother, Augustine, where there was a higher grade school kept by a Mr. Williams. Here he remained several years, receiving what would be called to-day a grammar-school education. After this sojourn with the folks at Bridges Creek, he returned home and attended a school in Fredericksburg, kept by the Rev. James Marye. There was no bridge over the river, and young Washington rowed his boat to and from school morning and evening in the roughest weather.

The copy and exercise books of Washington's school-days are fortunately preserved. In looking them over, one sees something of the talent and merit of the boy. They bear the marks of industry

and care. His handwriting indicates a
well-poised character, being "round, fair,
and bold," the lines running straight and
even. In these books much space is given
to legal forms, receipts, bills, leases, deeds,
wills, and such other matters required by
a business man in a community where
lawyers were few. Then we come to
pages of mathematical problems, with
well-drawn geometrical figures. Here is
a page where the lad has broken away
from his task, and the real boy nature
shows itself in crude drawings of birds,
human faces, and other indications of
school-boy pranks. Where is the boy who
but feels this "touch of nature," making
him akin with this Virginia youngster at
Ferry Farm?

Some one has said that the art of spell-
ing, like the use of the fork at table, must
be learned before one is fifteen, or it will

never be learned. Washington's class grade in the spelling-book was near the lower end of the list, but he led all in the department of mathematics, having a special talent and liking for this branch of learning. His ability, coupled with the influence of Lord Fairfax, secured for him, a few years later, the position of public land surveyor.

There was quite a stir in the home-nest of Madam Washington one day, just after George had turned his fourteenth year. It happened on this wise: The boy had been thinking about his future. He wanted a chance to try his wings, and finally decided that he would go to sea. His mother was startled when he made known to her his desire, and withheld her consent for some time. The request was, however, renewed, backed by the hearty indorsement of Lawrence Washington, in

whom George's mother had the utmost
confidence.

It is not strange that the boy became
possessed with this idea. He was a frequent visitor at Mount Vernon, now the
home of Lawrence Washington and his
charming wife. Lawrence himself had
served as a captain in a Virginia regiment
under Admiral Vernon in the attack of
naval and land forces upon Cartagena,
South America, in 1741. Doubtless
stories of this fight had been told many
times around the fireside at Mount Vernon. George had often watched the load-
ing of merchant ships at the river
wharves, and had looked longingly after
them as they swung into the current of
the river, and set their sails for the far-
distant ports of the Old World. There
was some of the blood of the old sea-kings
in him, and it was stirred by these sights

and sounds. More than this, there was a military streak running all through the Washington family, and George had inherited a double portion.

What was more natural to this strong, manly boy, with a life-record to make, than the determination to enter the British navy? His mother reluctantly gave her consent, and in 1746 Lawrence Washington obtained for George a midshipman's warrant in the British navy.

George was delighted with the outlook. Preparations for his leaving home were hurried along. His midshipman's uniform had been sent to him, and it is said the young sailor's luggage was on board a British man-of-war anchored in the Potomac. Look at the young hero as he stands dressed in his first uniform! The natty cap is very becoming, the enameled dagger-belt adds to his soldier bearing. With well-polished shoes, he is every inch a sailor.

Now comes in the demon of the play. Madam Washington had a lawyer brother by the name of Joseph Ball, living in London, who, hearing of the intention to send George to sea, wrote a strong letter to his sister opposing the scheme. The story goes on to say that this letter was received by Madam Washington the day before George was to sail. She had never lost her aversion to the plan, and now her brother's letter fixed her determination. At the last moment she entered her protest, carried her point, and saved her first-born from His Majesty's service, turning his life purpose in another direction. The familiar name George Washington means more to the world to-day than if it were listed among the names of Britain's greatest admirals! It was a sore trial

to the boy; but he took it without sulk-
ing, and went back to school for another
year, applying himself diligently to his
studies, giving special attention to land
surveying.

When he was fifteen years old, George
Washington passed through his first love
experience. As boy and man, he was very
susceptible to the charms of the fair sex.
Good-looking women were attractive to
him. There is something wrong in a man
when he is made up otherwise. But
Washington's juvenile love emotions
were set on the hair-trigger, and went off
very easily under the influence of a grace-
ful form and pretty face. As a school lad,
he was one day found "romping with one
of the largest girls." The tell-tale pages
of his journal inform us that, at the age of
fourteen he met a girl, while visiting his
half-brother Augustine, in Westmore-

land, with whom he fell deeply in love.
In the crude efforts of a young lover to
write poetry, he calls her his "Low Land
Beauty." For some reason this love affair
did not prosper. Either George was
jilted, or his shyness prevented him from
declaring his passion. He has told the
world of his flame in the pages of his journal. Here are a few lines of this boy
lover's lament:

"O ye gods, why should my poor, resistless heart
    Stand to oppose thy might and power
  At last surrender to Cupid's feather'd dart
    And now lays bleeding every hour
For her that 's pitiless of my grief and woes,
    And will not on me pity take."

Who or what this "Low Land Beauty"
was, no one is able to say.

Our young spark did not mope around
in gloomy solitude. He became more
diligent in study, and began some practical work in land surveying. Very soon

after the above lament we find him deeply interested in another "very agreeable young lady," whose charms, in a meas- ure, offset those of the "Low Land Beauty."

Although this boy lover describes some of these heart experiences in a motto poem—

> "'T was perfect love before,
> But now I do adore,"

it is stretching language to call them seri- ous affairs; they were such as any suscep- tible young fellow may pass through two or three times before the age of twenty years.

There is a very important feature of Washington's school life left for the clos- ing of this chapter. In one of his manu- script books we find this heading: "Rules of Civility and Decent Behavior in Com- pany and Conversation." Then follows a list of one hundred and ten rules in Washington's handwriting. His biographers have puzzled much over their origin, some insisting that he wrote them himself, others that he compiled them. Still others are of the opinion that he composed some of them, some of them he copied, and some he wrote down from the lips of his teachers and learned friends. Mr. Lodge, in his "Life of Washington," throws the latest light upon the subject, in the following words: "It has always been supposed that these rules were copied, but it was reserved apparently for the storms of a mighty Civil War to lay bare what may have been, if not the source of these rules themselves, the origin and suggestion of their compilation. At that time a little volume was found in Virginia, bearing the name of George Washington in a boyish hand on the flyleaf, and the date 1742. The book was entitled, 'The Young Man's Companion.' It was an English work, and had passed through thirteen editions. . . . It was written by W. Mather, in a plain and easy style, and treated of arithmetic, surveying, forms for legal documents, the measuring of land and lumber, gardening, . and many other useful topics, and it contained general precepts, which, with the aid of Hale's 'Contemplations,' may readily have furnished the hints for the rules found in manuscript among Washington's papers."

Whatever may have been their origin, we need only call attention to the rare moral insight of a fifteen-year-old boy, who would select such a code as the basis of his character and the guide of his life. Here are a few of them:

"Every action in company ought to be

with some sign of respect to those present."

"When you meet with one of greater quality than yourself, stop and retire, especially if it be at a door or any strait place, to give way for him to pass."

"Strive not with your superiors in argument, but always submit your judgment to others with modesty."

"Be not hasty to believe flying reports to the disparagement of any."

"Take all admonitions thankfully, in what time or place soever given; but afterwards, not being culpable, take a time or place convenient to let him know it that gave them."

"Think before you speak; pronounce not imperfectly, nor bring out your words too hastily, but orderly and distinctly."

"Speak not evil of the absent, for it is unjust."

"Make no show of taking great delight in your victuals; feed not with greediness; cut your bread with a knife; lean not on the table; neither find fault with what you eat."

"Be not angry at table, whatever happens, and if you have reason to be so, show it not; put on a cheerful countenance, especially if there be strangers, for good humor makes one dish of meat a feast."

"Let your recreations be manful, not sinful."

"Show not yourself glad at the misfortune of another, though he were your enemy."

"Wherein you reprove another, be unblamable yourself, for example is more prevalent than precept."

"Associate yourself with men of good quality, if you esteem your own reputation, for it is better to be alone than in bad company."

"Be not curious to know the affairs of others; neither approach to those that speak in private."

"Undertake not what you can not perform, but be careful to keep your promises."

"When you speak of God, or his attributes, let it be seriously in reverence."

"Honor and obey your natural parents, although they be poor."

"Labor to keep alive in your breast that little spark of celestial fire, called conscience."

CHAPTER VI.

LEAVING THE HOME NEST.

IN the year 1747 George Washington finished his formal school-training, and in the atumun of the same year he went to live with his brother Lawrence, at his country seat on the Potomac. Lawrence had named his home Mount Vernon, in honor of Admiral Vernon, under whom he had served as captain in the siege of Cartagena.

Happy is the youth who is favored with the privilege of companionship with a small group of well-poised, refined, and intelligent people! The circumstances of Washington's boyhood were especially favorable in this respect. No study of the formative period of his life is complete

which passes over in silence the school-
ing he received from the companionships
of men and women who were much older
than himself.

Lawrence Washington was an Oxford
graduate, and a finished gentleman. He
had married Anne Fairfax, daughter of
William Fairfax, who was the owner of
a plantation named Belvoir, a few miles
below Mount Vernon. William Fairfax
had been an officer in the English army,
and at one time governor of one of the
Bahama Islands. His home was the center of a social life renowned through the
neighborhood. The master of Belvoir
was a wealthy gentleman, of refined tastes
and educated mind. Between these two
homes there existed the closest social relations, and George Washington, visiting
Mount Vernon, found himself also among
the guests at Belvoir.

This acquaintance with the Fairfax family was a fortunate episode in the life of young Washington. One year previous to the autumn when George went to live with his brother Lawrence, Thomas Lord Fairfax, a cousin to William Fairfax, came to Virginia, and was staying for the time being at Belvoir. .He was a peer of the realm, an Oxford graduate, a member of the famous Spectator Club, and the owner of vast estates on the Northern Neck of Virginia. This distinguished Englishman was well on to sixty years of age when he first met the Virginia country boy, George Washington. They were mutually attracted to each other.

We can easily see how a boy of Washington's parts would become interested in such a man. Lord Fairfax was a past master of all the graces of fashionable high-bred English society, an instructive conversationalist, a friend of Addison, and at one time contributor to the *Spectator*. There were two experiences in his life which explain his presence in Virginia at this time: First, his ancestral estates in Yorkshire, England, had been sold to make good the debts of his spendthrift father; and, secondly, the titled gentleman had been jilted by a London belle, who suddenly found out that she could marry a duke, and therefore cast off her allegiance to his lordship. The Low Land Beauty and the London Belle may have had some part in forming those tender ties which bound these two souls into a lifelong friendship.

It is perfectly natural that the fancy of Lord Fairfax should be greatly smitten by the character of young Washington. Fairfax was a great lover of field sports, and in that phase of Virginia life Washington was to the manor born. Hunting, fishing, riding to the hounds, mountain climbing, fencing, boxing, swimming,— these were the recreations of Virginia boys in Washington's day. He could outrun any boy in the neighborhood; he had no peer for his age in horsemanship; he could throw a stone farther than any boy in Fredericksburg. A point on the Rappahannock is shown to the visitor where Washington once threw a silver dollar from one shore to the other. The quick-witted Yankee may say that a dollar went farther in those days than it does now, but the bright sally does not overthrow Washington's prowess as an athlete. He found pleasure in taking certain risks invariably connected with a sportsman's life.

> "No game was ever yet worth a rap
> For a rational man to play,
> In which no disaster or mishap
> Could possibly find its way."

Some pages of his diary fairly quiver
with the sportsman's enthusiasm,—a fox-
hunt, with the hounds in full cry, fleet
horses carrying their riders over ditches
and brambles and fences in hot pursuit
of the "little red rascal" racing for his
life. The picture is full of the strength,
vigor, and adventure of outdoor life. In
thinking of it one seems to catch some
of the strains of the old fox hunter's
songs:

> "The fox jumped over the parson's gate—
> We'll all go a-hunting to-day."

Boys, under such conditions, may be
the companions of men old enough to be
their grandfathers. The sportsman's democracy brings all sorts and conditions
of people together upon common ground.

Washington possessed a native prim-
ness, which acted as a counterpoise to his
love for field sports, and his self-control

prevented his love of adventure from lapsing into recklessness. He knew how to use the world without abusing it. His manly, courageous, straightforward nature highly recommended him to the esteem and affection of Thomas Lord Fairfax.

Through this friendship with the English lord, George Washington passed to his first practical work of self-support in life. The immense land estates of Lord Fairfax lying beyond the Blue Ridge Mountains comprised 5,700,000 acres. The eccentric bachelor had not come to Virginia simply to get rid of London life. He had much of the spirit of a true Colonist, and his mind was big with the purpose of opening up and settling the vast acres of rich land lying in the lovely valley of the Shenandoah, "the daughter of the stars." This great tract of country

was unexplored; its resources were unknown, except to a few wandering hunters and trappers, who had pushed westward into its solitudes, stimulated by the
demands of the fur-trade. It was known
among the Eastern settlements as the
"Great Woods." "Across it ran the great
war-trail of the Five Nations, passing
northeast and southwest." Lord Fairfax
had received information from the wandering trappers that pioneers from the
North were coming into the rich valley,
building their cabins, making settlements,
and maintaining a squatter sovereignty,
without troubling themselves about title-
deeds from the owner. The first thing to
be done was to obtain a survey of the
estate, thus enabling the owner to locate
special tracts of land, define their boundaries, and give legal titles. In the spring
of 1748, when Washington had just

passed his sixteenth birthday, Lord Fairfax appointed him as surveyor of the lands
beyond the mountains, lying in the "Great
Woods."

In March, 1748, George Washington
and George Fairfax, a son of William
Fairfax, with a few assistants, rode
through Ashby's Gap to the wild lands
where they began their work. Washington's diary records many of their experiences. Below we give a few quotations,
in which Washington speaks for himself:

"Friday, March 11th.—Began my
journey in company with George Fairfax,
Esq. We traveled this day forty miles, to
Mr. George Neavel's, in Prince William
County."

"Sunday, March 13th.—Rode to his
lordship's (Lord Fairfax's) quarter.
About four miles higher up the river, we
went through most beautiful groves of

sugar-trees, and spent the best part of the day in admiring the trees and richness of the land."

"Monday, 14th.—We sent our baggage to Captain Hites's, near Fredericktown (afterwards Winchester), and went ourselves down the river sixteen miles (the land exceedingly rich all the way, producing abundance of grain, hemp, and tobacco), in order to lay off some land on Cate's Marsh and Long Marsh."

Here is an account of his first night in a squatter's cabin:

"Tuesday, 15th.—Worked hard till night, and then returned. After supper we were lighted into a room, and I, not being so good a woodsman as the rest, stripped myself very orderly, and went into the bed, as they called it, when, to my surprise, I found it to be nothing but a little straw matted together, without

7

sheet or anything else, but only a thread-
bare blanket, with double its weight of
vermin. I was glad to get up and put
on my clothes, and lie as my companions
did. Had we not have been very tired, I
am sure we should not have slept much
that night. I made a promise to sleep
so no more, choosing rather to sleep in
the open air before a fire."

"Friday, 18th.—We traveled up about
thirty-five miles to Thomas Berwick's on
the Potomac, where we found the river
exceedingly high, by reason of the great
rains that had fallen among the Alleghanies. They told us it would not be ford-
able for several days, it being now six
feet higher than usual, and rising. We
agreed to stay till Monday. We this day
called to see the famed Warm Springs.
We camped out in the field this night."

"Sunday, 20th.—Finding the river not

much abated, we, in the evening, swam our horses over to the Maryland side."

"Monday, 21st.—We went over in a canoe, and traveled up the Maryland side all day, in a continued rain, to Colonel Cresap's, over against the mouth of the South Branch, about forty miles from the place of starting in the morning, and over the worst road, I believe, that ever was trod by man or beast."

This man Cresap was quite a character in that backwoods settlement. He carried on an extensive trade with the Indians, and was old-fashioned enough to believe that cheating them was wrong. Through his honesty he became one of the most influential frontiersmen of his time. His home was a backwoods hotel to all travelers. "He kept a big kettle ready, suspended to place a fire under, near a spring, for the use of the Indians, who often passed his place, and for that reason they called him the 'Big Spoon.'"

Washington's diary for Wednesday, March 23d, contains this record of a scene witnessed while a guest at Colonel Cresap's: "Rained till about two o'clock, and then cleared up, when we were greatly suprised at the sight of more than thirty Indians coming from war with only one scalp. We had some liquor with us, of which we gave them a part. This elevated their spirits; put them in the humor of dancing. We then had a war-dance. After clearing a large scape, and making a great fire in the middle, the men seated themselves around it, and the speaker made a grand speech, telling them in what manner they were to dance. After he had finished, the best dancer jumped up, as one awakened from sleep, and ran and jumped about the ring in a most comical manner. He was followed by the rest. Then began their music, which was performed with a pot half-full of water, and a deerskin stretched tight over it, and a gourd with some shot in it to rattle, and' a piece of horse's tail tied to it to make it look fine. One person kept rattling, and another drumming all the while they were dancing."

Washington was away from home just four weeks on this first outing trip as a surveyor. Lord Fairfax was so well pleased with his work, that he went at once to his estates in the Shenandoah, and built a lodge in the wilderness, naming it "Greenway Court." His intention was to build a great manor-house at this point, and live after the manner of an English earl. This intention, however, was never carried out. He lived to see his young friend famous, and to hear of the sur-

render of Lord Cornwallis at Yorktown.
He died December 12, 1781, at the age of
ninety years.

Washington's success as a surveyor
'soon won for him a wide reputation in his
profession.   Lord Fairfax was so well
pleased with the painstaking work of the
young man, that he obtained for him the
appointment of public surveyor, thus se-
curing for him steady employment.

For three years he devoted himself to
the work of his profession.   He was paid
according to the amount of work performed, earning from three to twenty dollars a day.   He had a keen instinct for
business, and with his wages he purchased
rich tracts of land here and there in the
neighborhood, laying the foundation of
the great estates owned by him in after
years.   It was a hardy, outdoor life he
lived during these years.   Rough, hard-

headed men were his companions. It
was a life beset with dangers, for there
was scarcely. a man on the frontier who
had not been shot at by an Indian. Sharp
ears and quick hands were required by
the men who pushed through the forests,
and marked the plantation boundaries for
the coming civilization. Englishmen are
proud of Wellington, and love to point
to the days when, on the playing-fields
of Eton, the young duke received the
training which made Waterloo possible.
Surveying in the "Great Woods" of Virginia, Washington developed the patience,
the courage, the perseverance, the zeal
shown by him in the terrible ordeals
through which he passed in the War for
Independence. The Revolution did not
produce George Washington: it simply
found him.

CHAPTER VII.

TROUBLE ON THE FRONTIER.

IN the year 1751 the current of Washington's life was turned in another direction from that of land surveyor. Lawrence Washington was seriously ill with consumption. His physician directed him to spend the coming winter in the Bahamas. Lawrence selected his brother George to go with him as nurse and companion. In September they set sail for the Sunny South. The trip was of no benefit to Lawrence, and George took the small-pox during his stay in the islands. It may have been a fortunate circumstance that he took the disease at this time, as he was thus delivered from the danger at a future period, when it was so

104

prevalent in the armies over which he was commander. This is the first and only time that the foot of George Washington ever touched any soil other than his native America.

The two brothers returned to Mount Vernon the next spring, and in July, 1752, Lawrence died, at the age of thirty-four years. His entire estate was left to his infant daughter, with the provision, in case of her death without issue, that it should revert to George, who was also appointed guardian of the child, and one of the five executors of the will. At this time he was twenty years old. The little girl died a few years after, and George Washington became the owner of Mount Vernon.

Before leaving for the Bahamas, Lawrence had secured for George the commission of major in the Virginia militia.

One year after this, Lieutenant-Governor Dinwiddie, the king's representative in Virginia, divided the Colony into four military districts, giving Washington charge of one, with the rank of major and adjutant-general. This position required him to inspect, organize, drill, and discipline the militia of the entire district, and be ready at any time for war on the frontier. It was a position of great responsibility for a mere youth of nineteen, and shows the high esteem in which his self-possession, judgment, and ability were held by the older men in the Colony.

This was a wise move on the part of the Colonial governor, for affairs on the western border looked threatening, and it became Virginia to gird herself for conflict.

At this period the French and English were the contesting parties for the posses-

sion of the New World. The English
Colonial possessions were along the Atlantic Coast. The Crown Charters of
these Colonies gave them possessions running west as far as the Pacific Ocean.
(No one at that time knew just how far
that was.) The English method of colonization was that of cutting away the
forest, planting farms, founding homes,
and building towns. As yet, these settlements had not gone beyond the Alleghany Mountains. Like Englishmen
everywhere, they wanted more elbow-
room, and a company of enterprising Virginians formed a corporation, known as
the "Ohio Company," for the purpose of
colonizing the fertile lands lying along the
Ohio River.

The French had entered the New
World through the two great waterways,
the St. Lawrence and Mississippi Rivers,

with military posts at New Orleans and Quebec. Their methods of colonization were chiefly by forts and trading-posts. They had determined to establish a great "despotic Catholic Empire" in the central portion of North America, and had made up their minds that the English, their old-time enemies, should not extend their domains west of the Alleghany Mountains. They had carried out their plan so far as to project a line of French forts and trading-posts, touching the modern sites of New Orleans, Natchez, Vincennes, Fort Wayne, Toledo, Detroit, Ogdensburg, and Montreal.

The French governor of Canada had sent his agents to take possession of the district claimed by the Ohio Company. They buried plates of lead at the junctions of the tributaries to the Ohio River, thus claiming authority over these regions, and warned the Indians not to trade with the English Colonists. It was a defiant challenge. Reduced to its simplest terms, it meant: "There are the Alleghany Mountains; beyond are the French possessions; thus far shalt thou come, and no farther."

It requires something more than bravado to cow an Englishman. He will claim his rights, even if he is to be shot at in the process. So the agents of the Ohio Company pushed westward over the mountains, and the French were very busy making the life of the English miserable all along the border. The French governor of Canada, Duquesne, had sent a military force into the debatable territory, charged with the twofold work of driving off English traders, and making alliances with the neighboring Indian tribes. They had taken possession of an English trader's quarters, raised the

French flag, and sent the occupants, as prisoners, to Canada.

Governor Dinwiddie, a brusque old Scotchman, combined private interests with official duties in his relations to the frontier. He was one of the twenty shareholders in the Ohio Company. He was also the king's representative as Colonial governor of Virginia. He sensed the situation in all its serious consequences. French supremacy on the frontier meant financial ruin to the Ohio Company, and blocked the progress of the English Colonies on the American continent. Very early in the history of the affair, Dinwiddie had communicated with the authorities in England, requesting them to outline a policy for his administration. The answer was prompt and direct. He was instructed to keep his hold upon the valley of the Ohio. Should the French continue trespassing in that quarter, he was "to require of them peaceably to depart." If they refused, "we do hereby strictly charge and command you to drive them off by force of arms."

The Colonial governor, acting according to instructions, put the stage in order for the play of diplomacy. He commissioned Major George Washington to be the bearer of a letter to the French officer on the disputed territory, requesting the French military forces to withdraw from the Valley of the Ohio. It was a task beset with many dangers. The route led through a trackless wilderness of five hundred miles. Streams swollen by early winter rains were to be forded, snow-covered mountains were to be crossed, wandering tribes of savage Indians were to be encountered and conciliated. More than this, the diplomatic work, after reaching the wily French authorities, was of a delicate nature, requiring a cool head, patient forbearance, and accurate judgment. It is a weighty testimony to the prudence, patience, courage, and judgment of young Major Washington, now twenty-one years of age, that he was selected as the Virginia envoy for this important mission.

On the 30th day of October, 1753, Washington received his commission from the governor, and on the same day set out on his journey from Williamsburg, the capital of Virginia. At Fredericksburg he stopped to say good-bye to his mother, and secure the services of Van Braam, his old fencing-master, as French interpreter. From thence he passed through Alexander and Winchester. In the latter he obtained the horses, tents, and other equipments needed for his journey. The real start on this mission was to be made from Willis Creek, the present site of the city of Cumberland, then the outpost of civilization.

Washington arrived at Willis Creek on November 14th, and made further selection of his companions for the journey— Christopher Gist, an experienced frontiersman; Davidson, an Indian interpreter; and four other men versed in the knowledge of the "Great Woods." Christopher Gist knew the way to an Indian village, called Logstown, on the Ohio River, seventeen miles below the present city of Pittsburg. After a week's travel, averaging ten miles a day, they arrived at the Monongahela River, striking it at a place called Turtle Creek. Here Washington divided his party, sending his baggage down the river in a boat under the care of two men. The other division

8

swam their horses over the swollen river,
and made their way across the country to
the point where the Monongahela and
Alleghany Rivers form the Ohio. The
overland company reached the forks of
the Ohio some time before the arrival of
the party in charge of the boat, and Washington employed the time in reconnoiter-
ing the country in the neighborhood. He
saw at once the importance of the point
where the two rivers joined to form the
Ohio, noting it as a strategic position for
future operations.

At the request of Washington, a council of Indian chiefs had been called at
Logstown by Shingis, the Sachem of the
Delawares. It was delicate work to
handle these Indians. The French agents
had been among them making alliances,
and had presented three of the chiefs with
"speech-belts," as tokens of friendship.

Washington explained to the council the orders which he had received from the governor of Virginia, and so conducted the interview that the Indians declared their preference for the English, and assured him that they would send back the "speech-belts" received from the French.

After a delay of five days with these adroit savages, Washington secured three chiefs and an old Indian hunter to accompany his party to Venango (now Franklin, Pennsylvania), the outpost of the French forces. On the 4th of December Washington arrived at Venango. His first view of this outpost must have stirred his blood. He there caught sight of the French flag floating over the captured quarters of an English trader. Captain Joncaire was the officer in charge of the post, to whom Washington presented himself, and made known his mission.

Joncaire informed him that his superior officer was stationed at Fort Le Bœuf, a point fourteen miles south of Lake Erie. He, however, strenuously endeavored to prevent Washington from going forward. He was lavish in his hospitality, but did all that diplomacy and whisky could do to alienate the Indians from the service of the English. There was every indication that the French had come into the Valley of the Ohio to stay. Joncaire, somewhat flushed over his wine, said in the presence of Washington: "It was their absolute design to take possession of the Ohio, and they would do it."

On the 7th of December, Washington left Venango, and pressed forward through sleet and snow sixty miles farther to Fort Le Bœuf, where he met the French commandant, M. de Sainte Pierre. Here again he was received with great hospitality, offset by the best work the Frenchmen could put in to induce the Indian chiefs to renounce their friendship for the English. Washington presented the letter from Governor Dinwiddie, and received from the French commandant his sealed reply.

The journey homeward was full of adventure and peril. The pack-horses gave out, and Washington, full of desire to report to his governor as quickly as possible, left the horses in charge of the other members of the company, while he and Gist, in Indian dress, pushed forward on foot through the woods.

On this return journey Washington was shot at by a treacherous Indian, who was acting as their guide. The trials and sufferings in getting across the Ohio River may be best told in Washington's own words: "There was no way of getting over but on a raft, which we set about, with but one poor hatchet, and finished just after sunsetting. This was a whole day's work; we next got it launched, then went on board of it, and set off; but before we were half-way over, we were jammed in the ice in such a manner that we expected every moment our raft to sink and ourselves perish. I put out my setting-pole to try to stop the raft, that the ice might pass by, when the rapidity of the stream threw it with so much violence against the pole that it jerked me out into ten feet of water, but I fortunately saved myself by catching hold of one of the raft-logs.

"Notwithstanding all our efforts, we could not get to either shore; but were obliged, as we were near an island, to quit our raft, and make to it. The cold was so extremely severe that Mr. Gist had all his

fingers and some of his toes frozen, and
the water was shut up so hard that we
found no difficulty in getting off the isl-
and on the ice in the morning, and went
to Mr. Frazier's."

Here Washington hired horses, and
pushed eastward over the Blue Ridge
Mountains, and in a few days arrived in
Williamsburg, presenting the letter of the
French commandant to the governor.
The letter was couched in diplomatic
form, but its meaning was easily understood. The French refused to withdraw
from the Ohio.

Washington's journal, kept while on
this trip, was considered of such importance, that the governor requested it for
publication, sending a copy to each of the
Colonial governors, and calling the attention of the home authorities to the contents of the book.

This journey was a failure, so far as the request of Governor Dinwiddie was concerned. It was a success in the revelation it made of the ability and character of Major Washington. He was known now as a wise organizer, a skillful reconnoiterer of military positions, a judicious treaty-maker with the Indians, and of dauntless pluck and courage in the presence of danger. He was Virginia's rising man.

CHAPTER VIII.

UNDER FIRE.

THE news of Washington's return, and the contents of Saint Pierre's letter, caused much excitement in Virginia. The authorities were brought face to face with war. The governor called for volunteers, enlisting officers were put at work, and war-drums were beating in many portions of the Old Dominion. The House of Burgesses presented much opposition to the governor's plans, and shied away from their responsibility of voting military supplies, by doubting the king's right to take possession of the Ohio Valley. By shrewd political management, the governor secured a grant of ten thousand pounds for the purpose of protecting settlers on the borders. He and his council issued orders to erect at once a fort at the junction of the Monongahela and Alleghany Rivers, the point selected by Washington during his trip as envoy to the French officer. Captain Trent, a trader and frontiersman, was sent forward, with such men as would enlist from the back settlements, to begin the construction of the fort.

A woodchopper and his ax awoke the echoes for quite a distance in the primitive forest; in fact, any sound made by a human being traveled quite easily on the Ohio at this time. This band of tree-cutters and log-hewers soon attracted attention by their work. Indian scouts brought the news to a French fort up the Alleghany River, and a bright, young officer quietly slipped one thousand French and Indians into canoes and boats, floated

down the Alleghany, seized the point, and
marched the Virginians out of their quarters, telling them he wanted to see no man
of them for a year. The French officer
then set to work enlarging and complet-
ing the captured fort, renaming it Fort
Duquesne.

As a reward for services rendered in
the expedition to the Ohio, Washington
was promoted to the position of lieutenant-colonel of a Virginia regiment, Colonel Fry commanding. There was a desire prevalent in high quarters to place
Washington first in command, but he protested, saying, "I have too sincere a love
for my country to undertake that which
may tend to the prejudice of it."

Through the winter months Washington was actively engaged in raising re-
cruits, drilling and disciplining them for
service. In this preparation for his first

military campaign, he found himself in
the midst of perplexities and hindrances,
which annoyed and embarrassed him all
through his military career—petty wran-
glings between the Colonial governor and
the House of Burgesses; sectional jealousies and narrow provincialism of the individual Colonies; prejudices between the
army officers who bore the king's commission and those who held their rank by
Colonial appointment; and the shiftless,
mutinous dispositions of many of the common soldiers.

In the midst of these exasperating difficulties, Washington left Alexandria on
the 2d day of April, 1754, with two companies of soldiers destined to support the
fort-building party on the Ohio. He
reached Willis Creek on April 20th, and
there learned of the capture of the fort by
the French. He immediately communi-

cated the news to Governor Dinwiddie, and wrote letters to the governors of Maryland and Pennsylvania, asking them to send forward troops. He did not wait for orders concerning his movements, but pushed on with his troops and military stores to Redstone Creek, a point on the Monongahela, about half-way to Fort Duquesne. By this plan he found employment for his men, and constructed a road over which the reserved troops could march more easily. By the latter part of May they had crossed the Alleghany Mountains, and had gone into camp at a place called Great Meadows. Washington described this place as "a charming field for an encounter."

The French and English had their scouts out in the direction of danger, and kept their respective headquarters well informed as to the movements of the enemy—that is the word now to be used in describing the relations between the English and French in America. It was the act of an enemy when the French took possession of the fort on the Ohio.

Washington had scarcely settled his camp at Great Meadows when he was informed by his Indian scouts that a party of French soldiers were on the march from Fort Duquesne, with the intention of giving battle to the English forces. Fearing a surprise, he did not wait for their arrival. His fighting blood was stirred, and he proposed now to do his duty as a soldier. Taking forty of his men, he pressed forward on a night march to surprise the enemy. He joined his Indian friends at sunrise on the morning of the 28th of May. He found the French concealed in a rocky ravine. The moment they saw Washington and his soldiers they sprang to arms. Washington gave the command to fire, and a brisk fight followed. The French commander, Jumonville, was killed, with nine of his followers, and twenty-two French were taken prisoners, and sent to Virginia. On the English side, one man was killed and two wounded.

After the engagement Washington marched back to Great Meadows, to await the arrival of re-enforcements, and erect fortifications for defensive action. Here an "independent company" from South Carolina joined him, and Colonel Fry's company of Virginia Volunteers came up without their colonel, Fry having died on the march. Washington was now commander of the whole military force, numbering something over three hundred men.

This skirmish in the backwoods of

Pennsylvania was a small affair considered in itself. Regarded in the light of issues involved, it was of momentous importance. It was the opening of a world-wide war drama. Two flags met that May-day on the field of Mars, the one bearing the Lilies of France and the other the Cross of St. George. By the order of Colonel Washington the war-dogs were unleashed, and their fierce yelping was heard on the continent of Europe for sixty years. In the fortunes of that long war France lost her possessions in America, England her "most flourishing Colonies," and America won her independence under the illustrious Washington. The war drama opened by the killing of Ensign Jumonville in a backwoods skirmish; it closed by paralyzing the arm of Napoleon at Waterloo.

Washington knew full well what developments would follow this first engagement with the French. He was in a dangerous position, far removed from the base of supplies, and confronted by an opposing force outnumbering his army four to one. His victory in the first fight was only a sugar-coating to the drastic medicine the French commander had prepared for him. He kept strenuously at work on the fortifications at Great Meadows, giving it the suggestive name of Fort Necessity.

On the 3d of July, nine hundred Frenchmen, besides many Indians, were drawn up in battle line along the border of the neighboring woods. Skirmishing went on all day, with more or less loss on both sides. In the evening Washington found his men exhausted. It had been raining all day. The rifle-pits were pools of water, and their powder was wet and

9

useless. The barb of battle must have been somewhat dull on the part of the French also. In the early evening the French commander requested the privilege of coming into the fort under a flag of truce, to present the terms upon which he would receive the surrender of Washington. This was declined by Washington. Later, however, the terms of surrender were accepted, and at midnight under a pelting rain, by the light of flickering camp torches, the articles of surrender were signed by both parties. The English were to march out of the fort the next morning with the honors of war. It must have been a humiliating experience on that 4th of July morning, 1754, when George Washington marched his surrendered forces out of Fort Necessity with drums beating and colors flying. It is worthy of note in this connection that this is the first and only time George Washington ever surrendered.

Washington's reputation at home did not suffer from this humiliating experience. His friends and neighbors looked upon him as an experienced soldier. The young colonel had been tested in his first campaign; he had stood under fire. The fortunes of war had brought him both the experience of victory and defeat. The House of Burgesses tendered to him and his officers a vote of thanks "for their brave and gallant defense of their country," and voted a bounty of four dollars to each of the soldiers under his command. The powder-stains on his face gave new dignity to his presence in official quarters, and emboldened him to talk some solid, common sense to the governor concerning military operations on the frontier.

After reporting to the governor at Williamsburg, Washington returned to his somewhat demoralized regiment stationed at Alexandria, where, with a cheerful spirit, he set about the work of drilling and recruiting the troops under his command, believing, with Hosea Biglow,

> "That civlyzation
> Doos git forrid,
> Sometimes upon a powder-cart,"

although at that particular moment it did not seem to be coming George Washington's way.

The young colonel had a supreme regard for his personal dignity. There was nothing uppish connected with this element of his character, but it was a serious matter to trifle with Washington's manhood. This sensitive nerve in the young Virginian had been touched by an order issued from the Home Government, whereby army officers holding the king's commission should rank above provincial officers. It further stipulated that "provincial generals and field officers should have no rank where a general or field officer holding a royal commission was present." This order occasioned endless jealousies among various military officers of the Colonial period, and threatened serious trouble in a campaign where regulars and provincial troops were engaged. Governor Dinwiddie hit upon a plan whereby he thought to obviate these difficulties. He divided the military forces of Virginia into ten independent companies of one hundred men each, placing over each company an officer ranking as captain. He offered the command of one of these companies to Colonel Washington. It was a stupid blunder; the Scotchman had reckoned without his host. No doubt the governor's intentions were good. He longed for harmony and peace among his army officers. But his action shows that he was deficient in that fine sense and pose of judgment requisite to appreciate the spirit and estimate the ability of such a man as Washington. To have accepted this proposition would have required Washington to resign his commission as colonel, and accept the lower rank of captain, rendering him liable to be commanded by any young ensign who perchance held the king's commission. There was not a drop of craven blood in the veins of Washington. He could not, in justice to his manhood, submit to this unmerited degradation, and men think the better of him for acting as he did. He therefore resigned his commission, and quietly retired to Mount Vernon.

In the meantime the English Government became more deeply interested in American affairs. "Carthage must be destroyed!" was Rome's cry when her Scipio drove Hannibal from the fields of Italy. The home Government had much of the same spirit in relation to the French in America. Two campaigns were organized against the French, one to proceed from New York and attack Nova Scotia; the other moving from Virginia against the French on the Ohio. The Colonies were to see fighting on the scale of English regulars.

Early in the spring of 1755 transports bearing two English regiments sailed up the Potomac River, and put the red-coated soldiers ashore at Alexandria. These troops were under the command of Major-General Edward Braddock, a brave, dashing, reckless Irishman.

One can easily imagine the thoughts

and feelings of Washington, as he stood
on the piazza at Mount Vernon, and
watched these military transports make
their way slowly up the Potomac. He
knew better than any military man in Virginia the route over which these troops
must march to the scene of action. His
knowledge of the country lying about the
forks of the Ohio would be invaluable to
a general proposing a military attack on
the French at Fort Duquesne. Further-
more, His Majesty's regulars were to be
accompanied on the expedition by Virginia militia, with a mixture of carpenters
and teamsters thrown in. It was a natural presumption on the part of Washington, mingled with no element of conceit,
that his knowledge and experience gained
in those regions should be placed at the
disposal of General Braddock. His interest in military affairs would also natu-

rally lead him to become a close student of such a campaign as the one now in preparation. He had read military books, he had commanded provincial soldiers, and he had seen some fighting, but he had never seen military operations conducted on such an extensive plan by soldiers skilled in the military discipline of the Old World. Upon Braddock's arrival in America, he wrote him a letter of welcome, and during all the days of preparation at Alexandria he was a frequent visitor at the British headquarters.

General Braddock and his officers set small store upon the lean, bony Virginia militiamen, and on many occasions were open in their demonstrations of contempt. Washington was, however, exempt from such treatment. This well-mounted horseman, riding through the British camp, attracted their attention, and called

forth their admiration. He combined the
strength of a backwoodsman with the
grace and dignity of an aristocrat. Six
feet two inches of such manhood com-
mands respect and attention anywhere.
Braddock took to the young Virginian,
and the outcome was just what George
Washington desired. General Braddock
invited him to join his military family as
aide-de-camp. Washington accepted the
position, becoming the most valuable
officer on the general's staff.

The story of Braddock's campaign and
defeat is known to every school-child.
The 9th day of July, 1755, is one of the
saddest in early American history. Two
thousand soldiers, with all their military
equipage, supplies, and artillery, forming a procession four miles long, were to
march five hundred miles through virgin forests and over trackless moun-

tains. After the outposts of civilization were passed, they were likely to be harassed by ambushed Indians and French enemies. The order had gone forth from the headstrong, quick-tempered commander that the campaign was to be conducted after the style of maneuvering armies in the open fields of Europe. It was an enterprise freighted with such hazard that even a Napoleon might have trembled at the undertaking. He spurned the advice of the experienced Washington and the sagacious Franklin concerning Indian ambuscades. "These savages," said Braddock, with a smile, "may indeed be a formidable enemy to raw American militia, but upon the king's regulars and disciplined troops, sir, it is impossible that they should make any impression."

At last the army began its march west-

ward. Its progress was slow. Elaborate
roads were to be made, and every delay
incident to transporting such a force by
such methods. At some places in the
march they occupied four days in getting
twelve miles. Braddock snubbed Washington for suggesting that pack-horses
would serve their purposes better than
army wagons.

At the ford of the Youghiogheny
Washington was taken sick with fever.
Braddock assigned him a guard, and left
him behind for rest and recovery, promising him, with his word of honor, that he
should be present and witness the battle.
Washington's recovery was speedy, and
he rejoined Braddock at the first ford of
the Monongahela, fifteen miles from Fort
Duquesne. The army must cross the river
again five miles below. They now began
to see traces of Indians and French scouts

in the neighborhood, and lost a picket
here and there by sharpshooters. Washington politely suggested the sending
ahead of the Virginia rangers, who knew
something about woods-fighting and Indian surprises. Braddock refused, and
set about awing the enemy by causing
his troops to go through the ceremony
of a military parade. On the 9th of July,
about noon, the order was given to cross
the ford. Washington was very much
impressed by the splendid appearance of
the army as it crossed the river. The
dark green of the forest contrasting with
the bright scarlet uniforms of the soldiers,
the midday sunlight flashing from the
bright bayonets and sword-hilts, the army
moving forward to the strains of the
Grenadier's March,—all these features of
that dreadful day were so firmly set in
the memory of Washington that he fre-

quently recalled them in the days when
he commanded the half-starved, poorly-
clad American patriots, who helped him
win our independence.

The army was scarcely across the river
when a man dressed in buckskin uniform
and wearing the badge of a French officer
came out of the woods. He looked at
the advancing army for a moment, then
turned his face towards the forest, and
waved his hat high over his head. It was
the signal for the concealed French and
Indians to open fire. The ambushed
enemy poured volley after volley into the
compact English ranks at point-blank
range. It was terrible carnage. The
officers stood to their posts like brave
men, General Braddock and Washington
bravest among them. Dead men were all
about them, and yet the English could
see no living enemy against whom to

direct their fire, so they shot wildly into the woods. General Braddock was learning at sad cost that trees and boulders could be utilized in battle with more telling results than orderly battle-lines firing in platoons. Five horses were shot under Braddock in quick succession, and finally a bullet pierced his lungs, and he fell. After that event the army broke in confusion and fled. Sixty-three officers out of eighty-five were either killed or wounded, and out of thirteen hundred men engaged, five hundred were killed or wounded. During the fight Washington did his utmost to carry out the plans of General Braddock. With furious energy and courage he threw himself into the midst of the slaughter. Three horses were shot under him, and his clothes were cut in many places by bullets. By his skillful management of the Virginia forces he saved what was left of the shattered army.

Aided by some of the officers, Washington carried Braddock to a place of safety, and watched with his wounded general until he died four days afterward. They buried the body near the scene of the encounter. The chaplain being wounded, Washington read the funeral service over his grave. The spot selected for the burial was in the roadway of the wilderness, where the wagons would obliterate every trace, thus preventing its discovery by the savage foes. After this sad ceremony, Washington turned his face homeward, arriving at Mount Vernon July 26th.

CHAPTER IX.

MARRIAGE AND MOUNT VERNON.

B RADDOCK'S defeat was an evil omen to the frontier settlements of Virginia. Savage Indians were now likely to press forward into the settlements, doing dreadful work with fire and tomahawk. With a few hundred militia, Virginia must protect her three hundred and fifty miles of frontier from the incursions of these savages. Washington was called to this task, and appointed commander-in-chief of the Virginia forces. It was a trying service, freighted with hardships and discouragements. Raising money by personal appeal, enlisting men through recreant recruiting officers, and enforcing discipline among ignorant and

10   145

trouble-making men—these were some of the difficulties to be encountered in the undertaking. He complains to the governor: "No order is obeyed but such as a party of soldiers or my own drawn sword enforces." In the midst of these drawbacks, he went on with coolness and courage doing his duty—"making an empty bag stand upright," which Franklin says is "hard."

The question of rank between king's and provincial officers was still a bone of contention. At Fort Cumberland there was a little fellow by the name of Dagworth, who, having held a king's commission, refused to obey Washington. This disagreement as to official rank resulted in a quarrel between Virginia and Maryland. Washington now determined to have this matter settled, and early in 1756 he set out for Boston on horseback.

The purpose of this journey was an interview with Governor Shirley, who was the
English commander-in-chief since the
death of General Braddock. Washington's desire was to obtain a king's commission as an officer in the army. In this
he failed. Governor Shirley, however,
gave him a written letter, stating that
each provincial officer must obey his superior in rank, even if that superior were
commissioned by another Colony.

Washington certainly intended to secure respect by the dignity of his personal
appearance on this seven-weeks' trip.
He was mounted upon one of his best
horses, his person was adorned with the
buff and blue uniform, a scarlet and white
cape was thrown over his shoulders, and
a gold-mounted sword swung at his side.
The trappings of his horse bore the Washington arms, in the style of the best Lon-

don saddlers. He was attended by two
aides dressed in full uniform, and two
servants clad in white and scarlet livery.
The handsome, young colonel, thus attended, must have attracted the admiring
attention of the people dwelling in the
Colonial towns and rural districts through
which he rode.

One of the marked traits in Washington's character was his fondness for fine
clothes. He was punctilious in his attention to fashionable garments. Wherever
he chanced to abide, the laundress and
barber were in great demand. The barber
found employment simply as a hair-
dresser, for Washington either shaved
himself or placed his person in the hands
of his valet for that service. It must not,
however, be understood that there was
any of the dandy about Washington. Far
from that. He selected and wore his

clothes on principle. He was a great ob-
server of facts, and it is a fact that a man
carries about with him a superior degree
of self-respect and wins a great measure
of respect from others by being well
dressed. It is an old saying that good
clothes have much to do with courtship.
Washington believed, other things being
equal, that good clothes went a great way
in accomplishing one's purposes in deal-
ing with one's fellow-men.

On his return journey he stopped in
New York, and received marked social
attention from the original "Four Hundred." He seems never to have taken to
New England, making no mention of Plymouth Rock or the Pilgrims. He did,
however, attend the meeting of the General Court held in the Old State House.
He does better by New York, bestowing
upon one of her fair daughters a deathless

memory through association with his name. During the round of social festivities given in his honor by the leaders of Knickerbocker society, his heart was captured, for the time, by Miss Mary Philipse, a young woman of great beauty and much wealth. Serious matters on the Virginia frontier demanded his presence, and he pressed hastily homeward, leaving the New York beauty to be won and wedded by Captain Morris, one of his fellow aides on Braddock's staff.

For three years Washington had a trying position at the head of the Virginia militia. In 1758 an overturn in the English ministry brought the reins of government into the hands of the great statesman, William Pitt. One of the Prime Minister's first acts in Virginia was to recall Governor Dinwiddie.. This circumstance, in its effect upon George Washington, was like a breeze of fresh mountain air coming into a ballroom. The new ministry set in motion a greater scheme, manned by abler men, to attack the French in their American strongholds. Another expedition was set in motion against Fort Duquesne under General Forbes. Washington was at the head of one of the Virginia regiments, still holding his commission as commander-in-chief of Virginia militia. Pitt's policy had broken the power of the French in the North, and the French occupants of Fort Duquesne had withdrawn to meet a need elsewhere, burning the fort upon leaving. All that remained for the Virginia expedition to do was to take possession. They erected a new fort, and raised over it the English flag, renaming the spot Fort Pitt.

The English were now in possession of

the Valley of the Ohio. Washington led his regiment back to Winchester, resigned his commission, and returned to Mount Vernon. This was in the latter part of December, 1758, and from that time until June 15, 1775, when the war-drums of the Revolution called him to a mighty task, Washington had no direct connection with military affairs.

In the early part of the last campaign against the French at Fort Duquesne there was an order placed in the hands of Washington by the quartermaster-general of the British army, instructing him to ride posthaste from Winchester to Williamsburg, and present before the governor and Council the humiliating condition of the Virginia troops as to their clothing and equipments. In the latter part of May, 1758, Washington and Billy Bishop, General Braddock's esteemed servant, set out on horseback for this journey. It was in Virginia springtide, and even the war-god must stand uncovered in the presence of his sweet sister, the love-goddess, in such rare days.

"In the spring a livelier iris changes on the bur-
    nished dove;
 In the spring a young man's fancy lightly turns
    to thoughts of love."

No man was ever more cautious in avoiding covert attacks than George Washington, and no victim ever rode more unconsciously into ambush than did this same George Washington that May-day about the hour of noon. The two horsemen had made their way through the country, passing the large estates and hospitable homes of the Virginia planters, and had arrived at a point on the Pamunkey River called Williams Ferry. Tradition says Washington was riding a splendid chestnut-brown horse, once owned by General Braddock. Scarcely had the ferry-boat touched the opposite shore when Major Chamberlayne, the hospitable proprietor of the grounds, recognized Washington, and insisted that he should come to his home and dine with him. Colonel Washington declined the invitation, stating that he was the.bearer of an important military message to the governor at Williamsburg. His friend pressed the invitation, saying that they were within a few hours' ride of the capital, and a good dinner would give zest to the remainder of their journey, closing his appeal with the assertion that there was a charming, young widow now visiting his home, whose company Washington would find entertaining. Virginia gallantry could no longer resist. Washington accepted the invitation, on the condition that after dinner his host would let him depart immediately. The charming woman proved to be Martha Dandridge, the widow of Daniel Park Custis, a gracious, intelligent, beautiful, and wealthy lady, living in a stately mansion near by, called the White House. She had married Mr. Custis when she was seventeen years of age, he being more than twenty years her senior. At the time of this meeting with Washington she was twenty-six years of age, his junior by three months, the mother of two children, a boy of six and a girl of four years. She had been one year a widow.

So much for background. The filling up of the foreground is alike interesting. Washington dismounted before the door of Major Chamberlayne's mansion, placing his horse under Bishop's care, strictly charging him to be ready for their further journey immediately after dinner. We will not stop over introductions and what took place during the pleasant hour at the table. Dinner over, the faithful Bishop was promptly on time with the horses, but Colonel Washington did not appear. Billy Bishop is a little nervous, and leads the horses up and down the green before the house, looking now and then askant at the windows, as if he would remind his master that time was up. Half the afternoon passes, and Washington still lingers within. "For once Washington loitered in the path of duty." We have uttered all that can be said of the impression Martha Custis made upon George Washington, when we state that the remainder of the day was spent in her company. It was sunset before he arose to depart, when Major Chamberlayne entered his protest by saying, "No guest ever leaves my

house after sunset." There is no record
of Washington uttering a word of complaint. He ordered Bishop to put the
horses back into the stable, and the night
was spent in the house of his host. Those
who ought to know say that the fair
widow and the handsome colonel lingered
"after the other guests had retired."

> "A ruddy drop of manly blood
> The surging sea outweighs;
> The world uncertain comes and goes, ·
> The lover rooted stays."

The next morning the sun was well up
towards the zenith before he was in the
saddle on his way to Williamsburg.

With soldier-like promptness Washington pressed his suit. On his return to
the frontier, he stopped at the White
House, obtained an interview with the
mistress, and, before they parted, Martha
Custis had promised George Washington

to become his wife. They were married
January 6, 1759. All the world knows
about that marriage. She satisfied Washington. She was the true mistress of his
heart till the day of his death. During
his life he wore a miniature portrait of
his wife hung from his neck by a golden
chain. In his letters he calls her "My
dear Patsy." In after years, when the
storm of battle roared about him, he spoke
of her as "the partner of all my domestic
enjoyments." His happiest days were
spent with her amid the home scenes of
Mount Vernon.

Soon after his marriage, Washington
took his wife to Mount Vernon, where he
set up housekeeping in a style commen-
surate with his social standing. He turned
his back upon war, but with the true instinct of a Virginian set his face towards
politics.

Six months before his marriage he had been elected a member of the House of Burgesses from Frederick County. His services here were so satisfactory to his constituency that he held this position for fifteen years, receiving each year a large majority of the votes cast. Upon taking his seat in the House for the first time, he received a hearty welcome, the Speaker making an address in which he presented to Washington the thanks of the House in honor of his military service. The sentiment was greeted with hearty applause from all present. The well-built colonel, measuring six feet in height, rose to respond. That was all he could do for that occasion. He was so confused that he simply stood there, blushing. and stammering, unable to utter an intelligent sentence. It took the House, however, better than any speech he might have made. The Speaker came to his rescue in the famous words: "Sit down, Mr. Washington; your modesty equals your valor, and that surpasses the power of any language I possess."

Washington's effective service was not in the line of speech-making; his worth was shown in sound judgment, careful study of facts, wonderful organizing skill, and spotless integrity. The source of Washington's masterly power in reading character and managing men has often been placed to the credit of a peculiar genius possessed by him for such work. The source of that power lies in another direction. It is revealed in his method of systematic work, in his habits of careful observation, and his wide range of experience. Early in life he was for years thrown in contact with all sorts and conditions of men, from the cultured circle of

Belvoir to the simple, rough life of the frontier. In the vigor of manhood he spent fifteen years in the study and management of men in the Virginia House of Burgesses. These experiences were not wasted on a man like Washington.

Here is a side-light showing his keenness of observation in some advice he gave to a nephew, who was about to take his seat in the House of Burgesses: "The only advice I will offer," he said, "if you have a mind to command the attention of the House, is to speak seldom but on important subjects, except such as particularly relate to your constituents; and, in the former case, make yourself perfect master of the subject. Never exceed a decent warmth, and submit your sentiments with diffidence. A dictatorial style, though it may carry conviction, is always accompanied with disgust."

During the period between 1759, the year of his marriage, and 1775, when he took command of the Continental army, Washington lived the life of a Virginia planter at Mount Vernon. These were his happiest years. This charming spot on the Potomac River was the goal of his earthly pleasure. There he held close companionship with agricultural life. Growing crops fascinated him. Late in life he wrote to a friend: "I think, with you, that the life of a husbandman, of all others, is the most delectable. It is honorable, it is amusing, and, with judicious management, is profitable. To see plants rise from the earth and flourish by the superior skill and bounty of labor, fills a contemplative mind with ideas which are more easy to be conceived than expressed." He loved horses, cattle, and dogs, and stocked his farms with the finest breeds. His business enterprises gener-: ally brought good returns; and barrels of flour and bales of tobacco, bearing the brand of "Geo. Washington," passed the custom-house officers unchallenged.

He was the master of Mount Vernon for forty-six years. During that period, twenty-three years were given to public service. Speaking of the losses on his farms, occasioned by his absence during the Revolution, he says: "To speak within bounds, ten thousand pounds will not compensate the losses I might have avoided by being at home and attending to my own concerns." For his service to the cause of liberty during the Revolution the ideal patriot declined any remuneration, requesting only the amount of his personal expenses.

Of all shrines sacred to the memory of Washington, Mount Vernon is the most suggestive. Other places renowned for his presence remind one of the hero, the warrior, the statesman—Mount Vernon suggests the man. Surrounded by those scenes, he played as a child. Back to those halls he came from his surveying trips. Through that doorway he led his bride. From that loved home he went forth with drawn sword in the cause of liberty. To its tranquil scenes he returned when the storm of war had passed, and his labors as President were over. The visitor to Mount Vernon feels the power of these memories. The whole place has an expectant look, as if the owner were only absent for a little while, and would return.

CHAPTER X.

STIRRING THE EAGLE'S NEST.

FROM the period of Washington's entrance into public life to the passage of the Stamp Act in 1765, in private thought and public action he was a loyal subject of the English king. He had grown up with a supreme respect for authority and a zealous regard for law, having no sympathy with radical enthusiasts whose zeal carried away their judgment.

Soon after the close of the French war, the Mother Country had adopted a policy in relation to Colonial affairs which savored much of oppression. Briefly stated, the policy was this: The American Colonies were to be a part of the great British

Empire so far as taxation and dependence went, but were to have no representatives in Parliament, and no share in legislation affecting them. The thoughtful leaders in Colonial politics looked upon this measure with serious apprehension. It was equivalent to the cry from the ship's lookout, "Breakers ahead."

The suspicious feeling on the part of the Colonies towards the authorities in England began to manifest itself very early in their relations with each other. The Colonial governors, generally speaking, were men who helped on the spirit of antagonism by their official arrogance. There was a constant warfare waged between them and their Assemblies, and this chronic opposition, coupled with later acts of injustice on the part of the English ministry, rapidly developed in America a public opinion looking towards independence.

Washington came thoughtfully and gradually under this influence. He loved his country with a patriot's devotion, and loathed injustice in his manly soul. He was forced to witness the object of his love treated with kingly oppression and the manhood of his fellow-citizens degraded. His first efforts to repair the injury were by way of remonstrance and compromise. But when all such proposals were met with disdain and refusal on the part of the English Government, he took the heroic stand and followed his duty home, boldly declaring: "Our lordly masters in Great Britain will be satisfied with nothing less than the deprivation of American freedom. Something should be done to maintain the liberty which we

have derived from our ancestors. No
man should hesitate a moment to use arms
in defense of so valuable a blessing, yet
arms should be the last resource."

If the demon of discord had been invited to preside over the deliberations of
the English ministry at this period, he
could not have suggested a policy more
detrimental to the peace of the American
Colonies than that adopted by King
George and his counselors. Space forbids
the enumeration and historic connection
of America's grievances during the period
previous to the Revolution. Some of
them, however, may be set forth in skeleton form.

During the French war, Colonial paper
money had been issued by the Colonies,
in order to meet the financial pressure
incident to the campaign. Scarcely had
hostilities ceased when the English Board

of Trade obtained an order from the English ministry declaring this paper money to be "no longer legal tender." This was the first blow from the millionaire fist ever given against the rights of the common people of America. It shocked Washington's sense of justice, calling from him the remark: "I fear this order will set the whole country in flames."

In 1761, English authority set itself in motion further to hector the Colonies by the enforcement of the Navigation Act. This act required all trade with the Colonies to be carried on through home ports, in British vessels. Sugar from the West Indies consigned to dealers in Maryland must first be shipped in English bottoms to some English port, and thence to the James or Potomac Rivers. Under such arbitrary measures, smuggling became a common practice. A Boston revenue officer made application to the court for a "writ. of assistance;" in other words, a general search warrant, permitting him to enter private houses, and search for smuggled goods. James Otis threw himself into the task of defeating this application before the court. In his appeal he used the famous sentence: "Arbitrary measures of this kind have cost one king of England his head, a second his crown, and they may yet cost a third his most flourishing Colonies." James Otis lost his case before the court, but his speech created such excitement and enthusiasm among those present, that the scene has been regarded as the opening act of the American Revolution.

Early in 1765 American indignation was kindled into flame by the passing of the celebrated Stamp Act by the British Government. This act required the

American Colonies to place a revenue stamp upon every newspaper or almanac published. They were also required upon all marriage certificates, wills, deeds, and other legal papers. These stamps varied in price from three pence to ten pounds. They were to be sold by officers duly appointed by British authority, and the money received used to pay British soldiers stationed in America to enforce the laws made by the English Parliament. .This act produced a general uprising among the Colonists from Massachusetts to Georgia. It is worthy of note that the first protest coming from a representative body in America had its origin in Virginia, the Colony hitherto most loyal to the crown. Secret societies known as the "Sons of Liberty" were formed in most of the Colonies, whose members were under secret oath to resist the oppressive law.

Stamp officers were burned in effigy, and the boxes containing the stamps were burned or cast into the sea. It was evident the Stamp Act could not be enforced in America, and the English Government, after prolonged debate, repealed the law, still insisting upon the right to tax the Colonies. Speaking of this Act after its repeal, Washington said: "The consequence would have been more direful than is generally apprehended, both to the Mother Country and the Colonies."

The repeal of the Stamp Act amounted to nothing so far as the principle at stake was involved, for it was saddled with a rider, reasserting the *right* of Parliament to impose taxes on the Colonies. It was much like scraping the coat from the tongue of a fever patient, with the hope of thus curing him of disease. England's contention in the matter of Colonial tax-

ation was an affair of the pocket-book.
America's resistance was rooted in the
principle of justice.

Soon after the repeal of the Stamp Act,
the British Ministry ordered a duty to be
placed on certain articles shipped to
America. This was described as an in-
direct tax, and it was taken for granted
that the Americans would submit to it,
for some such intimation had been made
in the debate on the repeal of the Stamp
Act. It was evident from this action that
the snake had been scotched and not
killed. The Colonies responded to the
order by boycotting the articles mentioned, and Washington in his orders for
English goods for Mount Vernon carefully avoided sending for articles specified
in the tariff list. This action touched the
commerce of the Mother Country, and
that has always been a sensitive nerve in

British national life. The import duties were soon repealed on all goods shipped to America, with the exception of the duty on tea. This exception was made on the ground that a tea tax would be the least objectionable to the Colonies, because it touched fewer people, and at the same time would maintain the right of Parliament to tax the Colonies; that is to say, the insignificance of the tax on tea would protect it from opposition. It is said that tea was so little known among the Colonies at this time that when a Virginia gentleman gave his overseer a pound of the delicious shrub as a present to his wife, she, thinking it was some new-fashioned greens, boiled the whole of it in a pot with a big ham.

The Colonists, however, were not caught napping. American patriotism did not lose sight of the principle in-

volved, and declared its defiant opposition
in words that could not be misunderstood—"The right to take one pound im-
plied the right to take a thousand."

Protests were unavailing, and in 1773
vessels loaded with tea by the East India
Company were sent to Boston, New York,
Philadelphia, and Charleston. The presence of these ships in American waters
produced among the people an outburst
of indignation destined to shake the continent. Everywhere the question of landing these cargoes of tea was met with
an emphatic No! In Charleston, the only
place where a ship discharged her cargo,
the tea was stored in a damp cellar and
spoiled. In Boston more heroic measures
were adopted. Mass-meetings, attended
by thousands of citizens, were held in Fan-
euil Hall and the Old South meeting-
house. Samuel Adams rocked the cradle

of Liberty to the tune of an intense patriotism.   A letter from the patriots of
Philadephia exhorted the men of Boston
to stand firm, saying, "Our only fear is
lest you may shrink.   May God give you
virtue enough to save the liberties of your
country!"

In one of these mass-meetings, held in
the Old South Church, John Rowe stood
up, and said: "Who knows how tea will
mingle with salt water?"   The remark was
greeted with great applause.   The patriots
had exhausted all legal methods and used
their wisest words of petition to prevent
the landing of the tea.   Governor Hutch-
inson sent his last word of refusal to the
meeting.   Samuel Adams then arose, and
quietly but distinctly said: "This meeting
can do nothing more to save the country."
Soon afterwards a war-whoop was heard
outside the church, and fifty stalwart citi-

zens of Boston dressed as Mohawk Indians marched down to the wharf, boarded
the three tea-ships, broke open three hundred and forty-two chests of tea, and flung
their contents into Boston Harbor. The
next morning Dorchester Beach was
fringed with salted tea, carried there by
wind and tide during the night. It was
a costly trimming with which Boston
adorned the shore of her picturesque
suburb.

The "Tea Party" cost the East India
Company much; it was yet to cost Boston
more. England demanded compensation
for the destruction of the tea; Boston refused, although Benjamin Franklin, writing from London, suggested payment.
The answer was promptly returned,
"Do n't pay for an ounce."

General Gage was ordered to Boston
with four regiments of British regulars,

who closed her port and ruined her commerce. Her distress met with universal sympathy in the Colonies. Most of the Assemblies held meetings, and voted that Boston was "suffering in the common cause." Droves of cattle and sheep were being driven from all directions to the relief of the city. Gifts of clothing, food, and money, carried by ox-carts and farm wagons, were brought to the martyr town. Heading a subscription list for the purpose of feeding the unemployed working classes of the town was the name of George Washington, with a gift of fifty pounds.

In the Virginia Convention, called to select delegates to the first Continental Congress, Washington was chosen as one of their representatives. He there uttered some words which Mr. Lynch declared to be "the most eloquent speech that ever

was made." Speaking of the distressing
oppression of Boston, he said: "I will raise
a thousand men, subsist them at my own
expense, and march them to the relief of
Boston." When George Washington,
"the silent man," had anything to say, he
said it so that men understood his meaning.

England had so heartlessly stirred the
eagle's nest in America that the young
Colonial birds could stand it no longer,
but took wing and soared to independence. Mother England intended other results to come out of this treatment, but
Divine Providence used her folly to accomplish the very end she sought to prevent.

A Continental Congress, made up of
representatives from all of the Colonies,
was first proposed by the Sons of Liberty
in New York. This proposition was ac-

cepted by the Colonies, and on the 5th
day of September, 1774, the first Continental Congress met in Carpenters' Hall
in the city of Philadelphia. Washington
was one of the seven delegates from Virginia, his name standing third on the list.
This was the first time the representative
men of the Colonies had ever met face to
face in convention. Washington said little
in this Congress, but spent much time in
studying the men, getting at their ideas
and purposes through conversation and
friendly visits. This Congress sat for fifty-
one days, occupying the time in debating
and discussing the vital questions pertaining to American affairs. In speaking of
the *personnel* of this body, Patrick Henry
said: "If you speak of solid information
and sound judgment, Colonel Washington is unquestionably the greatest man on
the floor."

The second Continental Congress met
at Philadelphia, May 10, 1775. War-
clouds were now in the sky. Washington
came to this Congress wearing the blue-
and-buff uniform of a Virginia colonel.
What his purpose was in appearing on the
floor of Congress clad in military garb no
one knows. It has been suggested that
it was his way of saying the hour for fighting had come: "Like the war-paint of an
Indian, his soldierly dress was a figure of
speech, to tell that the time for compromise had passed by, and the question must
be settled, not by words, but by blows."
The battle of Lexington had been fought,
and an army of sixteen thousand patriots
had gathered in Cambridge for the defense of Boston. Congress was called
upon to adopt this army, and select a
commander-in-chief for its head. The
choice of a commander seemed a simple .

matter to John Adams. He moved that
Congress adopt the army at Cambridge,
and said he had "but one gentleman in
mind, a gentleman from Virginia, who
was among us, and very well known to
all of us; a gentleman whose skill and experience as an officer, whose independent
fortune, great talents, and excellent universal character, would command the ap-
probation of all America, and unite the
cordial exertions of all the Colonies better
than any other person in the Union."
Washington's modesty was touched by
these words, and before Mr. Adams had
finished this tribute, he quietly arose and
left the room. Silence prevailed in the
House for a few moments; then the vote
was taken, and Washington was unani-
mously elected commander-in-chief of the
Continental army.

On June 19, 1775, his commission was

signed, and by the 21st of the same month
he was on his way to Boston. He had
ridden but twenty miles on his way when
a horseman met him bearing the news of
Bunker Hill. "Did the militia fight?"
was his first question. Receiving the decisive "Yes!" he exclaimed, "Then the
liberties of the country are safe," and rode
forward to one of the greatest tasks ever
imposed on mortal man.

> "The day is broke, my boys, push on!
> And follow, follow Washington.
> 'T is he that leads the way, my boys,
> 'T is he that leads the way.
>
> When he commands, we will obey,
> Through rain or sun, by night or day,
> Determined to be free, my boys,
> Determined to be free."
>   *—Revolutionary Song.*

CHAPTER XI.

COMMANDER-IN-CHIEF AND PRESIDENT.

W ASHINGTON'S ride from Philadelphia to Boston during those early summer days of 1775 created a profound impression among the inhabitants of the country through which he passed. Enthusiastic citizens escorted him from one town to another. The nearer he came to New England, the more earnest he found the people in their patriotism. This ride was a telling object-lesson to the people of the Colonies, proclaiming the dignity and sterling character of the leaders engaged in the service of liberty. No man, after seeing that cavalcade, escorting the great Virginian to his post of duty, could speak sneeringly of a movement led by such men as George Washington.

Washington's mind must have been occupied with serious thoughts. He was on his way to take charge of an insurgent army. There were some terrible examples of the failure of such work in the past. The bloody scenes of the Jacobite rebellion, from 1715 to 1744, were still fresh in the English mind, and the memory of Culloden field, where the courageous Highlanders were defeated and butchered by the regulars of the British army was a threatening prophecy of what English regulars might do in these struggling Colonies, beginning·in Boston. He was to draw his sword against the strongest military power in the world. He was to contend against a nation from which he had inherited his own fighting blood. There was still vitality enough in tyranny

to strangle the cause of liberty in the New
World. His foe possessed the advantage
of an ancestral aristocracy, guarded by a
titled nobility. A pompous State religion would throw its mighty influence
across his path. The throne of despotism
was buttressed by the wealth, the learning, and the art of ages. Men of genius
stood ready to do the bidding of royalty.
And, worst of all, the lacerated form of
Liberty, for which he was contending, had
been branded in high quarter with the
crime of regicide. Out of such a past,
into the untried future, Washington
looked on the morning of July 3, 1775,
when, on Cambridge Common, under the
"Old Elm," he placed his hand on the hilt
of his sword, drew it from the scabbard,
and raised it in the presence of the army
and the people. Such a venture involved
business risk, home risk, personal risk;

yea, the hazard of everything but *self-respect;* yet the consciousness of devotion to a just cause led him to count life itself as nothing compared with the great boon of freedom, for which he was now contending.

> "One self-approving hour whole worlds outweighs
> Of stupid starers, aud of loud huzzas,
> And more true joy Marcellus, exiled, feels
> Thau Cæsar with a Senate at his heels."

It should be noticed, in this connection, that the hectoring injustice on the part of the British ministry, which threw the American Colonies into revolt, was not the work of the common people of England. The unreasonable acts of Parliament were not passed without vigorous opposition on the part of some of England's most sagacious men. The world might have been spared the American Revolution had not the English Government been practically in the hands of two young and inexperienced men—George III and his prime minister, Lord North. The king was thirty-two years of age, Lord North his senior by five years. Lord North was simply the henchman to his sovereign, and this young representative of the House of Hanover was a narrow-minded ruler, who mistook obstinacy for heroism, and personal whims for wise political policies. A little sound statesmanship on the part of these two men might have prevented the appeal to arms.

The condition of the provincial troops before Boston sorely tried the military spirit of Washington. The lack of discipline was demoralizing. Short enlistments made possible the reduction of the army in critical times, and the want of ammunition paralyzed any forward movement in the way of attack. He patiently went to work to bring order out of this confusion. He had experienced many like embarrassments while commanding Virginia troops in the days of the French war; but he had hoped to find more public spirit and better discipline among the New England levies. In his confidential letters he does not mince words in describing the state of affairs. He complains of their lack of effective organization: "The people of this Government have obtained a character which they by no means deserve. Their officers, generally speaking, are the most indifferent kind of people I ever saw. I dare say the men would fight very well (if properly officered), . . . although they are an exceedingly dirty and nasty people. . . . It is among the most difficult tasks I ever undertook in my life to induce these people to believe there is or can be any danger till the bayonet is pushed at their breasts. Not that it proceeds from any uncommon prowess, but rather from the unaccountable kind of stupidity in the lower class of these people, which, believe me, prevails too generally among the officers of the Massachusetts part of the army, who are nearly of the same kidney with the privates." There may have been something of the Virginia cavalier in these words; but, however that may be, Washington's trials at this critical time were extremely harassing. He was forced to stand by and witness the disbanding of a part of his army through short enlistments. He was pressed with the necessity of recruiting another army in the presence of an enemy liable to give battle any day. There was just cause for complaint when a man of Washington's courage and nerve could write: "Could I have foreseen what I have experienced and am likely to experience, no consideration upon earth could have induced me to accept this command." This feeling concerning New England troops soon left him, and afterwards he wrote strong words of commendation on the soldierly qualities of New England men.

Six weeks after his arrival in Boston Washington had his plan for defense completed. During the winter he employed the time by gathering military stores, arms, and ammunition for the use of his troops. For six months the two camps were within a mile of each other, and did little but guard duty. Quiet was maintained on the part of the English by the memory of Bunker Hill, and the Continentals rested on their arms for lack of powder.

By March following Washington had

succeeded in getting sufficient powder to warrant an attack upon the British. During the winter he had brought cannon through the forests from Ticonderoga, and in one night threw up fortifications and mounted his guns on Dorchester Heights. The British had been caught napping. The fortification of this strategic point completed Washington's line of defense about Boston. The town and its harbor were now in full range of the cannon on Dorchester Heights. This move filled the English officers with alarm, and on the 17th of March eight thousand British troops and nine hundred Tory citizens of Boston found it convenient to take a sea-voyage to Halifax, leaving behind them all their medical supplies and instruments, two thousand cannon, and a great quantity of military stores, powder, muskets, gun-carriages, and small arms. To this day the citizens of Boston are called from their slumbers at six o'clock on the morning of the 17th of March, by the belfry bells ringing out in memory of "Evacuation-day."

Washington took possession of the town, establishing his headquarters in Mrs. Edwards's boarding-house, the place formerly occupied by General Howe, the British commander. There is an amusing story told concerning Washington's stay in this house. One day he took the little granddaughter of his hostess on his knee. and asked her which she liked the better, the red coats or the provincials. "The red coats," was the reply. "Ah, my dear," said the commander, with a twinkle in his eye, "they look better, but they do n't fight. The ragged fellows are the boys for fighting." •

Washington was not so carried away

with his bloodless victory, as to neglect
the significance of the future. He knew
the English Government would send a
greater army against the Colonies, and he
surmised the scene of action would be
transferred from Boston to New York.
Leaving a sufficient number of troops in
Boston to garrison the town, he marched
with his army to New York, and on the
13th of April, 1776, he began organizing
the defense of that city by recruiting the
army and erecting fortifications.

At this time he was fully convinced
that there was no possibility for America
to obtain her freedom by remaining a subject of the British crown. He was ready
for independence. The war was now to
be carried on with that end in view. On
the 4th of July, 1776, Congress issued the
Declaration of Independence. Washington ordered this immortal document to

be read before the army. It was received with great enthusiasm, both by the soldiers and citizens in the Colonies.

Not long after the issue of the Declaration of Independence, a large British fleet dropped anchor in New York Bay. This meant war on a more extensive scale than had ever before been witnessed on the American continent. The British Lion was aroused, and determined to strike a decisive blow.

Now followed a year of humiliating disasters to the American cause. Washington's army was driven from Long Island; Fort Washington on the Hudson was forced to surrender more than three thousand soldiers, opening the great river to the navigation of English men-of-war. The British forces chased Washington's depleted army through the Jerseys far across the Delaware River. In the midst

of these defeats Washington never lost
heart. After crossing the Delaware, he
stopped for a time in his retreat, and, like
a wounded lion furious to deal a dying
blow, he recrossed the Delaware in the
darkness of a winter night, and won the
great victory of Trenton. In January,
1777, he went into winter quarters at
Morristown with an army of less than four
thousand men. This was the end of his
first campaign.

In the opening spring he regained the
Jerseys, coming off the victor in several
engagements, but was soon driven out
by the pressure of the British force.
Brandywine was a British victory, and
defeat was measured out to him at Ger-
mantown. The British army had gained
possession of Philadelphia, and driven the
Continental Congress farther South.

In the winter of 1777-78, Washington

went into quarters at Valley Forge. In that terrible winter the sufferings of the Continental army were indescribable. Yet the Ideal Patriot, George Washington, did not yield to despair. In 1776 he had an army of forty-seven thousand men; in 1777 it was less than twenty thousand. The division with Washington at Valley Forge was shelterless and poorly clad; blankets were so scarce that terrible winter that many soldiers were forced to stand all night by times around the camp-fires to keep from freezing. At one time more than one hundred soldiers had not a shoe to their feet, and their line of march could be traced by the blood-marks which their naked feet left in the snow.

During that winter Washington offered a prize for shoes made from untanned hides. For months he had been calling the attention of Congress to his needs, yet that body were indifferent to his appeals. "Hogsheads of shoes, stockings, and clothing were lying at different places on the roads and in the woods perishing for want of teams or money to pay the teamsters," yet Congress failed to vote measures for his relief. The only action put forth by that body at this time was the vote passed removing both the commissariat and quartermaster-general's department from his control.

In the midst of these difficulties there arose an ugly plot on the part of some of his trusted generals to displace Washington as commander-in-chief. This conspiracy was known as the "Conway Cabal." The treason of Benedict Arnold and his desertion to the enemy was the bitterest part of that cup of suffering from which Washington was forced to drink during the dark days of the Revolution. Arnold was a man for whom Washington cherished a deep affection. When he learned that his friend had played the part of a traitor, great sobs broke from his distressed heart, and all night long he paced his room in company with his bitter thoughts.

The only ray of bright light which shone through these dark days upon the American cause was the good news that the British General Burgoyne had been trapped at Saratoga by General Gates, surrendering over five thousand regulars. But even this victory brought with it something more than joy to the heart of Washington, for it carried with it a certain feeling of distrust on the part of the country as to the efficiency of Washington's leadership. Even New England became suspicious of him, and Samuel Adams, noble patriot that he was, wanted demo-

cratic rotation in the office of commander-
in-chief, suggesting the hiring a general
by the year.

Yet hope deferred and threatening disaster did not make Washington heart-
sick. Through all these trials he quietly
kept steadfastly to his purpose. He had
faith in his cause, anchoring his hopes to
his favorite quotation, " 'T is not in mortals to command success."

Cheerful news soon came from over the
sea. The big brain of dear old Benjamin
Franklin was planning for the American
cause at the French court, and after the
surrender of Burgoyne, France acknowl-
edged the independence of the United
States of America, promising help to the
cause of American freedom in money,
men, and munitions of war. The period
of the American Revolution has a literature of its own. There is not space

enough in this volume to tell fully the
story of the war, and, if there were, it
would be presumption on the part of the
writer to attempt it. For a full and fasci-
nating account of those heroic days the
reader is referred to the charming pages
of Mr. John Fiske's "American Revolution." It is no disparagement to American leaders and soldiers to say that, without French intervention, the cause of
America could not have been carried to
victory. American gratitude associates
very tenderly the name of the dashing
young French nobleman, Lafayette, with
that of her great patriot, Washington.

At last the end came. At Yorktown
the blow was struck which closed the war.
On the 19th of October, 1782, the formal
surrender of the British forces under Lord
Cornwallis took place, and on the 19th
day of April, 1783, just eight years to a

day after the battle of Lexington, peace was proclaimed between the two nations in the contest. The terms of the surrender of Lord Cornwallis specified that the British flag was not to fly, and American music must not be played. The band selected an old English air, called "The World Turned Upside Down." The title of the piece of music must have been descriptive of the feelings of the English prime minister, Lord North, for, upon hearing of the surrender of Cornwallis, he exclaimed, "O God, it is all over!"

Washington's first order after the surrender was a call for a day of public thanksgiving and praise to God. "Divine service is to be performed to-morrow in the several brigades and divisions. The commander-in-chief earnestly recommends that the troops not on duty should universally attend with the seriousness of deportment and gratitude of heart which the recognition of such reiterated and astonishing interpositions of Providence demand of us."

In the interim between the surrender at Yorktown and the final disbanding of the army there were many serious difficulties besetting the young Nation. Washington still kept his hand on the helm, and guided the contending factions into peaceful waters. Congress had made no satisfactory provision for the back pay of the soldiers. The men who had stood with Washington through those trying years of war were angered at this show of ingratitude. An anonymous letter had been sent through the army threatening serious action if their wages were not provided for. Washington saw the danger to the success of the Nation in this threat, and immediately called the officers and men before him, reading to them a long, pleading, and telling speech full of the noblest patriotism. He had proceeded but a little way in his reading, when he paused for several moments, slowly took his spectacles from his pocket, and, in the process of adjusting them, feelingly said: "Gentlemen, you will pardon me for putting on my glasses. I have grown gray in your service, and I now find myself growing blind." It was a magnetic touch of sentiment, and deeply affected his audience, causing them to listen with fixed attention to his words and to heed his appeal.

When the time came for disbanding the army, Washington, with his officers and a few of the troops, were in New York. He was about to return to private life at Mount Vernon. Gathering his officers about him in the old Fraunce Tavern in Broad Street, he said, with deep emotion in his voice: "I can not come to each of you to take my leave, but shall be obliged if each of you will come and take me by the hand." General Knox, who stood nearest, was the first to extend his hand to his great chief. With tears in his eyes, Washington took the hand of his much-loved comrade in arms, drew him towards him, and kissed him. All the others were greeted with the same affectionate parting. He was then escorted to the North River, where he crossed by ferry and proceeded to Philadelphia. After such a scene, let the American people hear no more of the statement that the Father of his Country was not an affectionate man. On the 23d of December, 1783, Washington presented his resignation as commander-in-chief, and again became a private citizen. The next day he returned to his home at Mount Vernon.

American political affairs were in a deplorable condition at the close of the Revolution. The Colonies were free from the English yoke, but there was a sad lack of union between them. War had for a time bound them together in a common interest, but upon the establishment of peace their old sectional jealousies were tearing them asunder. "Thirteen staves, and ne'er a hoop do not make a barrel," was the quaint way in which one of their statesmen described their condition. Men called "Virginia or Carolina my country." They had not yet come under the spell of that patriotism represented by the word America. The Nation had as yet no existence. Our studious historian, Mr. Fiske, says: "It is not too much to say that the period of five years following the peace of 1783 was the most critical moment in all the history of the American people." In this serious time Washington was again called from his loved home, and placed at the head of the Nation.

In 1787 the great Constitutional Convention was called. Virginia sent George Washington at the head of her delegation. When the Convention assembled in Philadephia, Washington was chosen as its presiding officer. This august body of Nation-makers was composed of fifty-five members. They assembled day after day for a period of four months, discussing and formulating the great principles of the Constitution of the United States of America. Mr. Bancroft calls them "the goodliest fellowship of lawgivers whereof this world holds record." And of their work—the Constitution of the United

States of America—Mr. Gladstone declares that it is "the most wonderful work
ever struck off at a given time by the
brain and purpose of man." This Convention adjourned on the 17th of September, and on the 19th the great document
was published throughout the country,
and finally accepted by the States.

The question of selecting a President
for the new Government was the first
claiming the attention of the people. The
Constitution provided for the election of
an Executive who should be called "the
President of the United States." When
the time came for the election of such
an officer to direct the course of the Nation, all minds turned to Washington, and
he was chosen President without a dis-
senting vote. He held this high office for
two terms, extending over a period of
eight years. Through all these years he

guided the Ship of State with that per-
sistent wisdom and justice which had
characterized his administration of all
matters connected with his fellow-men,
drawing the lightning from the clouds of
faction, and conducting it harmlessly to
the ground. The renowned hero of the
battle-field became the successful and wise
administrator in the times of peace.

On the 3d of March, 1797, Washington's term of office as President expired,
and again he congratulated himself that
he was permitted to put great duties aside,
and resume the quiet life of a husbandman
at Mount Vernon. It was not a quiet life,
however, for he was a man with a world-
wide fame, and was forced to pay the incident penalty. Visitors beset him from
all quarters; artists from over the sea came
to paint his portrait; curiosity-seekers
thronged Mount Vernon until even Vir-

ginia hospitality was taxed to its utmost endurance.   .

This did not last long, for the Ideal Patriot was near his end.   On December 12, 1799, this man, who was proof against the deadly arrows of savage Indians and the whizzing bullets of the battle-field, was stricken at last by the unerring aim of the archer Death.   He had spent the day riding over his farms, while "rain, hail, and snow" were "falling alternately, with a cold wind."   When he returned home he was chilled through.   The next day he kept in-doors most of the time, "and complained of having a sore throat."   "He had a hoarseness, which increased in the evening; but he made light of it, as he would never take anything to carry off a cold, always observing, "Let it go as it came.'"

The following day the doctor was

called, and found his patient in much dis-
.tress. He could "swallow nothing," "ap-
peared to be distressed, convulsed, and
almost suffocated." Later in the day he
gave directions concerning his will, and
then said, "I find I am going," and, "smil-
ing," remarked, "that, as it was the debt
which we must all pay, he looked to the
event with perfect resignation." To Dr.
Craik he said: "I die hard, but I am not
afraid to go. I believed from my first
attack that I should not survive it; my
breath can not last long." Thanking his
attendants for their tender care, he requested them to trouble themselves no
more; "but let me go off quietly." His
last words were, " 'T is well."

"About ten minutes before he expired,
his breathing became much easier; he lay
quiet, . . . and felt his own pulse. . . .
The general's hand fell from his wrist,"

Between the hours of ten and eleven o'clock that night his noble spirit passed beyond the scenes of earth's turmoils and cares into the rest and peace of the Better Land.

"There's a star in the West that shall never go
   down,
  Till the records of valor decay;
We must worship its light, though 't is not our
   own,
  For liberty bursts in its ray.
Shall the name of a Washington ever be heard
  By a freeman, and thrill not his breast?
Is there one out of bondage that hails not the
   word
  As the Bethlehem-star of the west?"

CHAPTER XII.

WASHINGTON'S VISION OF THE WEST.

AT daybreak on the morning of the 13th of September, 1759, General Wolfe and his gallant English soldiers found themselves in possession of the fateful Plains of Abraham. Montcalm, the French general who held Quebec, the citadel of Canada, was thunderstruck when informed that the English were on the heights; but the contest was on, and there was fought the memorable battle that decided whether Englishmen or Frenchmen were to take the leadership of American affairs.

"With the triumphs of Wolfe on the Heights of Abraham began the history of the United States," is the estimate Mr.

Green, the historian, places upon this event. Our own charming historic writer, Mr. John Fiske, says: "The triumph of Wolfe marks the greatest turning-point as yet discoverable in modern history." Another writer, describing how the English cause that day was the cause of America, and especially of the great West, eloquently says: "Montcalm stood for the old *régime*, Wolfe for the House of Commons; Montcalm for the alliance of king and priest, Wolfe for *habeas corpus* and free inquiry; Montcalm for the past, Wolfe for the future; Montcalm for Louis XV and Madame de Pompadour, Wolfe for George Washington and Abraham Lincoln."

Prior to the battle of Quebec the entire Mississippi Valley, from Canada to the Gulf of Mexico, was under the dominion of France, the English possessions comprising only a skeleton of Colonies lying along the Atlantic Coast. When, amid the crash of Wolfe's musketry that day on the Plains of Abraham, victory perched upon the English banner, a changed destiny awaited the American people. There it was settled forever that the resources and possibilities of America were to be developed by New England, and not by New France. "Wolfe's victory," says Bancroft, "one of the most momentous in the annals of mankind, gave to the English tongue and the institutions of the Germanic race the unexplored and seemingly infinite West and North."

The possession of the great West was the principal stake for which France and England had contended here in America during more than half a century. In 1753, six years previous to the fall of

Quebec, George Washington, then twenty-one years of age, comes before us for the first time in this struggle between France and England for the dominion of the great West. About this time a number of Maryland and Virginia Colonists formed an association known as the Ohio Company, organized for the purpose of colonizing the Ohio Valley. Lawrence Washington, George Washington's oldest brother, was the manager, and Augustine, another brother, was one of the charter members, This scheme of planting English Colonists in the Ohio Valley was a subject of frequent conversation at Mount Vernon; for we must remember that both the Massachusetts and Virginia charters, given by James I, included the whole country from the Atlantic to the Pacific. One can easily imagine how this project took possession of the mind of

young Washington. He seems to have
had a vision, which revealed to him the
importance of the West to the future of
America, and to it he ever afterwards
yielded unhesitating obedience.

During the period when the Ohio
Company was receiving such attention
from the intelligent and enterprising men
of Virginia, through the influence of Lord
Fairfax, an intimate friend of the family,
George Washington received his commission as public surveyor. In this capacity
he made many journeys into the wilderness beyond the Blue Ridge Mountains,
receiving his first experience in wood-
craft and the exposure of camp-life, becoming acquainted with Indian tribes and
studying their methods of guerrilla warfare. In reading the diary kept by him
during these expeditions to the West, it
is manifest that the magnitude and im-

portance of that vast domain made a profound impression upon him, and one in-
stinctively feels that he believed himself
called to take an active part in the work
of developing this great frontier.

The French in Canada kept a keen eye
on this colonizing scheme of the Ohio
Company, and determined to enter their
protest against the westward march of the
English Colonists from Virginia. They
gathered stores and munitions of war
upon Lake Erie, and in 1753 began the
erection of a line of forts from Lake Erie
to the Ohio River.

This advance of the French on the territory claimed by the English created
alarm among the Virginia Colonists.
Governor Dinwiddie resolved to challenge the right of the invaders, and request them to withdraw. He selected as
his envoy for this important commission

Major George Washington, who by this time had received the appointment of adjutant-general of the Virginia militia. The order was received by Washington on the last day of October, 1753. A close student of those heroic days declares that "Nothing in all Washington's career is more remarkable" than the fact that, while a mere boy of twenty-one, he was "chosen for such a difficult and dangerous enterprise." It was this rough Scotch Colonial governor, Mr. Parkman suggests, "who launched Washington on his illustrious career."

On the 16th of January, Washington returned to Williamsburg, and waited on the governor with the letter from Saint Pierre, the French commandant. His journal, carefully kept on this trip, was considered of such importance at the time, that the governor ordered it to be printed and circulated in England and America. This was George Washington's first appearance in print, and it is interesting to note that it was in connection with his earliest services in the struggle for the great ' West on the part of the French and English Colonists.

The French gave little heed to the warning of the Virginia governor, Saint Pierre sending word to him by Washington that he was there by the orders of General Duquesne, the governor of Canada, which orders he should obey with "exactness and resolution." In defiance of Dinwiddie's challenge, a force of one thousand soldiers was pushed still further down the river from Venango to the point where the Alleghany and Monongahela unite to form the Ohio; the sixty men sent there by the Ohio Company to build a fort were driven out, and the French army took possession of the post, and built a strong fort themselves, naming it Fort Duquesne, after their governor.

This position—the site of the present city of Pittsburg—had been selected by Washington himself, who regarded it as the key to the whole territory in dispute. Such an aggressive move on the part of the French was interpreted as a declaration of war by the Colonists in Virginia, and Washington, now lieutenant-colonel, in command of Virginia troops was sent to the scene of action to carry on the war. The battles of Great Meadows, Fort Necesity, and Braddock's Field have already been described in this volume; they are here mentioned to show that in the military career of George Washington his first service was rendered to save the Western territory for the future development of the United States of America.

When peace spread her wings over the land after the fall of Quebec, Washington was just settling down at Mount Vernon as a married man. In the midst of the duties pertaining to the life of a husbandman, he was still earnestly engaged in maturing plans for the colonization of the Western border. Through his influence large tracts of land were awarded the officers of the army in consideration for their services in the French war. He projected schemes looking toward the importation of Germans for the settlement of the lands lying in the great western woods. He was personally interested in an extensive "land boom" for the West. And this not simply for money-making purposes. There was nothing discreditable to Wash-

ington in his land speculations. "He contemplated an extensive public benefit, as
well as private advantage." In this respect he was the forerunner of that American public spirit which has united private
enterprise and public good in the development of the continent. Washington was
convinced, by a practical sagacity which
seldom failed him, that the course of empire in America was westward. In this
the Virginia statesman and soldier antici-
pated, by some hundred years, the famous
dictum of Horace Greeley—"Go west,
young man."

During the stormy days of the Revolution, Washington's mind was confronted by other problems, and his active
interest in Western matters subsided
somewhat; yet even during the trying-ex-
periences of that conflict we catch
glimpses which show that the West still

held a place in his thought. In case the
cause of the patriots was lost on the Eastern battle-fields, he had determined to
withdraw his army into the virgin forests
of the Alleghany Mountains, and there
defy and hector King George by maintaining a guerrilla warfare. When it was
intimated during the darkest days of the
Revolution that the emperor of Russia
had joined hands with the British to crush
the cause of liberty, Washington was
asked one day by a serious patriot, "If this
be true, and we are driven from the Atlantic border, what is to be done?" "We will
retire to the Valley of the Ohio, and there
be free," was the prompt answer.

When the war was over, and peace
with England was established, Washington turned again to his vision of the westward march of the United States of America; for it must be remembered that be-

fore the close of the war he repeatedly referred to the "United States" as an empire in process of development; he saw it
by faith until he felt it as fact. It has been
truly said that, with the exception of
Hamilton, no man of his time grasped
the magnificent future opening before the
nation as did Washington.

In 1784, Washington, in a letter to
Benjamin Harrison, governor of Virginia,
outlines and urges the plan for making
easy the trade relations between the East
and the West. This plan was to open up
a route westward by the Potomac River.
He calls Harrison's attention to the fact
that the Potomac connection is nearer to
tidewater than the St. Lawrence by one
hundred and sixty-eight miles; nearer
than the Hudson River by one hundred
and seventy-six miles. "The Western
States," he argued, "stand as it were on a

15

pivot; the touch of a feather would turn them" either towards the Mississippi or the Atlantic Coast in the outlet for their trade.

Sectional and State jealousies were the *bête noire* of Washington's public life, and he strenuously urged the sinking of all such differences in the broad scheme of National federation. In private letter and public proclamation he sought to indoctrinate the people with the importance of National union. In reading his able Farewell Address, one is impressed with the truth that his deepest solicitation was not a question of the peaceful relations between the North and the South—although even then slavery was a threatening cloud on the horizon of the future. The storm-center, as Washington saw it, hovered over the line dividing the East from the West. To obviate any such con-

flict, he set himself to develop the policy
of easy and free communication between
the two sections of the country, binding
them together by river courses, public
canals, and national roads. The Potomac
Canal Company, pushing its waterway
through the Alleghanies, uniting the
Western Reserve with the Eastern Sea-
board States, was the foreshadowing of
our present great trunk-lines of railroads,
speeding over Western prairies, climbing
with their white plumes the Rocky Mountains, uniting the East and the West
under one standard of national, commercial, and social life.

Washington's policy in relation to sectional America is worthy of the profound-
est attention by the political students of
the present hour. In our political and
commercial life to-day the line of cleav-
age runs in the same direction; splitting

sounds are heard in our national elec-
tions; and sectional prejudices, aired by
political demagogues, create dangerous
combinations in our body politic. Washington was the first statesman of his time
to grasp the Continental idea of the American Commonwealth. His words to Lafayette tersely express his thought on the
subject: "The honor, power, and true interest of this country must be measured
on a continental scale." The first definite
plan for the formation of Western States
is found in a letter written by Washington
to James Duane, member of Congress
from New York. This letter bears the
date of September 7, 1783, and suggests
the laying out of two new States beyond
the Ohio River. The State lines suggested by Washington bear a striking re-
semblance to the present shape of the
great States of Ohio and Michigan. It is

not improbable that in looking at the lines of conformation in these States, we have before us Washington's first plan for the division of the western territory into representative Commonwealths.

When we take into account the petty jealousies and sectional bitterness existing between the thirteen Colonies, the hesitancy and obstinacy on the part of some in coming into the Union under the Constitution, and then compare this pragmatic provincialism with Washington's noble vision of America's future, we heartily indorse the sentiment of Edwin D. Mead: "Never does Washington seem more truly the Father of his Country, never does the Great First in War stand so close to the Great First in Peace."

CHAPTER XIII.

WORDS OF WASHINGTON.

IN presenting these sayings of Washington, the writer humbly claims the privilege of calling attention to the marvelous insight of the man, concerning the principles which were to be worked into the political and social life of the nation.

In Washington's day the history of republics presented a gloomy picture; among the great nations of the world Liberty meant little more than a word derived from the dead language of the Romans. It was a sorry past from which to draw inspirations for future democracy.

Yet in this hour Washington was the nation's prophet. Like Moses, he enunciated the principles and designated the materials out of which the American Commonwealth was to rise, "according to the pattern shown him in the mount." His thought is clothed in the stately English common to his time, a period when love-letters were written after the manner of State documents. In his letters to his mother he invariably addressed her as "Honored Madam." Nevertheless, his sentences clearly express his thought; they are not garnets and rubies gathered from the sands of sparkling streams, but solid cubes of granite quarried for the foundations of empire. Even to-day a policy is relieved of much debate if it can be shown that it had the approval of Washington.

Washington's favorite quotation was the line from Addison:

"'T is not in mortals to command success."

THE END OF GOVERNMENT. ✓

The aggregate happiness of society, which is best promoted by the practice of a virtuous policy, is, or ought to be, the end of government.

DEMOCRACY.

It is among the evils, and perhaps not the smallest, of democratic governments, that the people must *feel* before they will *see.* When this happens, they are roused to action. Hence it is that those kinds of government are so slow.

AMERICA.

Great Britain thought she was only to hold up the rod, and all would be hushed.

PEACE POLICY.

My policy, in our foreign transactions, has been to cultivate *peace with all the world;* to observe the treaties with pure

and absolute faith; to check every devi-
ation from the line of impartiality; to explain what may have been misappre-
hended, and correct what may have been
injurious to any nation; and having thus
acquired the right, to lose no time in ac-
quiring the ability, to insist upon justice
being done to ourselves.

Would to God the harmony of nations
were an object that lay nearest to the
hearts of sovereigns, and that the incen-
tives to peace, of which commerce and
facility of understanding each other are
not the most inconsiderable, might be
daily increased!

Washington's words of advice to a
nephew, who was about to take his seat in
the House of Burgesses:

"The only advice I will offer," said he,
"if you have a mind to command the at-

tention of the House, is to speak seldom but on important subjects, except such as particularly relate to your constituents, and, in the former case, make yourself perfect master of the subject. Never exceed a decent warmth, and submit your sentiments with diffidence. A dictatorial style, though it may carry conviction, is always accompanied with disgust."

"Honesty in States, as well as in individuals, will ever be found the soundest policy."

"Discourage vice in every shape."

The prevalent belief that Washington was cold in the realm of friendly affections shows how his private life has been neglected and misunderstood. Strip his letters of the pompous literary style of his day, and some of them are very tender. Here is one to Lafayette, after parting from the French Patriot, containing the tender pathos of real life: "In the moment of our separation upon the road as we traveled, and every hour since, I have felt all that love, respect, and attachment for you with which length of years, close connection, and your merits have inspired me. I often asked myself, as our carriages separated, whether that was the last sight I should ever have of you. My fears answered, yes. I called to mind the days of my youth, that they had long fled to return no more; that I was now descending the hill I had been fifty-two years in climbing; and that, though I was blessed with a good constitution, I was of a short-lived family, and might soon expect to be entombed in the mansion of my fathers. These thoughts darkened the shades, and gave a gloom to the picture, and consequently to my prospects of ever seeing you again."

THE CURRENCY.

I am well aware that appearances ought to be upheld, and that we should avoid as much as possible recognizing, by any public act, the depreciation of our currency. . . . It is our interest and truest policy, as far as it may be practicable, on all occasions, to give a currency and value to that which is to be the medium of our internal commerce.

SPECULATORS IN THE CURRENCY.

This tribe of black gentry work more effectually against us, than the enemy's arms. . . . It is much to be lamented, that each State, long ere this, has not hunted them down, as pests to society and the greatest enemies we have to the happiness of America. I would to God that some one of the most atrocious in each State was hung upon a gallows, five times as

high as the one prepared by Haman. No
punishment, in my opinion, is too great
for the man who can build his greatness
upon his country's ruin.

Commerce and industry are *the best
mines* of a nation.

I have been writing to General Knox
to procure me homespun broadcloth of
the Hartford fabric, to make a suit of
clothes for myself. I hope it will not be a
great while before it will be unfashion-
able for a gentleman to appear in any
other dress. Indeed, we have already
been too long subject to British prejudices.

WAR AN EVIL.

My first wish is to see this plague of
mankind banished from the earth, and the
sons and daughters of this world employed in more pleasing and innocent
amusements than in preparing imple-

ments, and exercising them for the destruction of mankind.

MOTTO.

Perseverance and spirit have done
wonders in all ages.

When we assumed the soldier, we did
not lay aside the citizen.

FOREIGNERS.

It does not accord with the policy of
this Government to bestow offices, civil
or military, upon foreigners, *to the exclu-
sion of our own citizens.*

PRISONERS OF WAR.

I am informed that General Putnam
sent to Philadelphia, *in irons,* Major
Stockton, taken upon the *Raritan,* and
that he continues in strict confinement.
I desire that if there is a necessity for confinement, it may be made as easy and com-
fortable as possible to Major Stockton

and his officers. This man, I believe, has been very active and mischievous; but we took him in arms, as *an officer of the enemy*, and by the rules of war we are obliged to treat him as such, and *not as a felon*.

KNOWLEDGE.

Do not forget that there ought to be a time appropriated to attain knowledge, as well as to indulge in pleasure.

FOREIGN EDUCATION.

It has always been a source of serious regret with me to see the youth of these United States sent to foreign countries for the purposes of education, often before their minds were formed, or they had imbibed any adequate ideas of the happiness of their own!—contracting too frequently not only habits of dissipation and extravagance, but *principles unfriendly to repub-*

lican government and the true and genuine
liberties of mankind, which thereafter are
rarely overcome.

NATIONAL UNIVERSITY.

That a National University in this
country is a thing to be desired, has always been my decided opinion; and the
appropriation of grounds and funds for it
in the Federal City has long been contemplated.

— FRIENDLY ADVICE.

The opinion and advice of friends I receive, at all times, as a proof of their
friendship, and am thankful when they
are offered.

To correspond with those I love is
among my highest gratifications.

The company in which you improve
most will be least expensive to you.

Men's *minds* are as variant as their

faces. Let your heart feel the afflictions and distresses of every one. Let your hand give in proportion to your purse, remembering always the estimation of the widow's mites.

SLAVERY.

There is not a man living who wishes more sincerely than I do to see a plan adopted for the abolition of it; but there is *only one proper and effectual mode* by which it can be accomplished, and that is by *legislative* authority. This, as far as my suffrage will go, shall never be wanting.

I never mean, unless some particular circumstance should compel me to it, to possess another slave by purchase, it being among my first wishes to see some plan adopted by which slavery in this country may be *abolished by law.*

Upon the decease of my wife, it is my

16

will and desire that all the slaves whom I hold *in my own right* shall receive their freedom.

PATRIOTISM.

I was summoned by my country, whose voice I can never hear but with veneration and love.

When my country demands the sacrifice, personal ease must always be a secondary consideration.

The love of my country will be the ruling influence of my conduct.

I require no guard but the affections of the people.

TRUST IN GOD.

I shall rely, confidently, on that Providence which has hitherto preserved and been bountiful to me.

I believe that man was not designed by the All-wise Creator to live for himself alone.

REFUSAL OF PECUNIARY COMPEN-
SATION.

When I was first honored with a call into the service of my country, then on the eve of an arduous struggle for its liberties, the light in which I contemplated my duty required that I should renounce every pecuniary compensation. From this resolution I have in no instance departed; and being still under the impression which produced it, I must decline, as inapplicable to myself, any share in the personal emoluments which may be indispensably included in the permanent provision for the Executive department; and must accordingly pray that the pecuniary estimates for the station in which I am placed may, during my continuance in it, be limited to such actual expenditures as the public good may be thought to require.

DOMESTIC LIFE.

You may believe me, my dear Patsy, when I assure you, in the most solemn manner, that, so far from seeking this appointment,* I have used every endeavor in my power to avoid it, not only from my unwillingness to part with you and the family, but from a consciousness of its being a trust too great for my capacity; and that I should enjoy more real happiness in one month with you at home, than I have the most distant prospect of finding abroad, if my stay were to be seven times seven years.

I can truly say, I had rather be at Mount Vernon with a friend or two about me, than to be attended, at the seat of Government, by the officers of state and the representatives of every power in Eu-

---

* Commander-in-chief.

rope. I shall hope that my friends will visit and endeavor to keep up the spirits of my wife as much as they can; for my departure will, I know, be a cutting stroke to her.

ADVICE ON MATRIMONY.

A woman very rarely asks an opinion, or requires advice, on such an occasion till her resolution is formed; and then it is with the hope and expectation of obtaining a sanction—not that she means to be governed by your disapprobation—that she applies. In a word, the plain English of the application may be summed up in these words: "I wish you to think as I do; but, if unhappily you differ from me in opinion, my heart, I must confess, is fixed, and I have gone too far *now* to retract."

"Went a fox-hunting with a gentleman who came here yesterday. . . . After a very early breakfast found a fox just back of Muddy Hole Plantation, and after a chase of an hour and a quarter with my dogs and eight couple of Doctor Smith's (brought by Mr. Phil. Alexander) we put him into a hollow tree, in which we fastened him, and in the Pincushion put up another fox, which in an hour and thirteen minutes was killed. We then, after allowing the fox in the hole half an hour, put the dogs upon his trail, and in half a mile he took to another hollow tree, and was again put out of it; but he did not go six hundred yards before he had recourse to the same shift. Finding therefore that he was a conquered fox, we took the dogs off, and came home to dinner."—*Excerpt from Diary.*

In a letter to Lafayette, written from Mount Vernon, he says: "Free from the bustle of a camp and the busy scenes of·

public life, I am solacing myself with those tranquil enjoyments of which the soldier, who is ever in pursuit of fame; the states- man, whose watchful days and sleepless nights are spent in devising schemes to promote the welfare of his own, perhaps the ruin of other countries—as if this globe was insufficient for us all; and the courtier, who is always watching the countenance of his prince in hopes of catching a gracious smile, can have very little conception. I have not only retired from public employments, but I am retir- ing within myself, and shall be able to view the solitary walk, and tread the paths of private life with heartfelt satisfaction. Envious of none, I am determined to be pleased with all; and this, my dear friend, being the order of my march, I will move gently down the stream of life until I sleep with my fathers."

RURAL EMPLOYMENTS.

My time is now occupied in rural amusements, in which I have great satisfaction, and my first wish is (although it is against the profession of arms, and would clip the wings of some of our young soldiers, who are soaring after glory) to see the WHOLE WORLD IN PEACE, and the inhabitants of it AS ONE BAND OF BROTHERS, striving who should contribute most to the happiness of mankind.

Nothing is more a stranger to my breast, or a sin that my soul more abhors, than that black and detestable one, of ingratitude.

INTEMPERANCE.

My chief reason for supposing the West India trade detrimental to us was, that rum, the principal article received from thence, is the bane of morals and the parent of idleness.

This I am certain of, and can call my conscience, and what I suppose will be a still more demonstrative proof in the eyes of the world, my Orders, to witness, how much I have, both by threats and persuasive means endeavored to discountenance gaming, drinking, swearing, and irregularities of every other kind.

GIN-MILLS.

I apprehend it will be thought advisable to keep a garrison always at Fort Loudoun; for which reason I would beg to represent the number of tippling-houses in Winchester as a great nuisance.

GAMING.

Gaming of every kind is expressly forbidden, as being the foundation of evil and the cause of many a brave and gallant officer's ruin.

Avoid gaming. This is a vice which is

productive of every possible evil; equally injurious to the morals and health of its votaries. It is the child of Avarice, the brother of Iniquity, and the father of Mischief. It has been the ruin of many worthy families, the loss of many a man's honor, and the cause of suicide. The *successful* gamester pushes his good fortune, till it is overtaken by a reverse; the *losing* gamester, in hopes of retrieving past misfortunes, goes on from bad to worse, till, grown desperate, he pushes at everything, and loses his all.

RELIGIOUS MAXIMS.

It is impossible to account for the creation of the universe, without the agency of a Supreme Being.

It is impossible to govern the universe, without the aid of a Supreme Being.

It is impossible to reason, without arriving at a Supreme Being.

I feel now, as I conceive a wearied trav-
eler must do, who, after treading many a
painful step with a heavy burden on his
shoulders, is eased of the latter, having
reached the haven to which all the former
were directed, and from his housetop is
looking back and tracing, with an eager
eye, the meanders by which he escaped the
quicksands and mires which lay in his
way; and into which none but the All-
powerful Guide and Dispenser of human
events could have prevented his falling.
When I contemplate the interposition of
Providence as it was manifested in guid-
ing us through the Revolution, in preparing us for the reception of a General Government, and in conciliating the good-will
of the people of America towards one
another, after its adoption, I feel myself
oppressed and almost overwhelmed with a
sense of the Divine munificence.

I earnestly pray that the Omnipotent Being, who has not deserted the cause of America in the hour of its extreme hazard, may never yield so fair a heritage to anarchy or despotism.

The propitious smiles of Heaven can never be expected on a nation that disregards the eternal rules of order and right, which Heaven itself has ordained.

I commend my friends, and with them the interests and happiness of our dear country, to the keeping and protection of Almighty God.

Whilst just government protects all in their religious rites, true religion affords government its surest support.

Of all the dispositions and habits which lead to political prosperity, religion and morality are indispensable supports. In vain would that man claim the tribute of patriotism, who should labor to subvert *these great pillars of human* HAPPINESS, these firmest props of the duties of men and citizens. The mere politician, equally with the pious man, ought to respect and cherish them. A volume could not trace all their connections with private and public felicity. Let it simply be asked, Where is the security for property, for reputation, for life, if the sense of religious obligation desert our oaths, which are the instruments of investigation in courts of justice?

The want of a chaplain, I humbly conceive, reflects dishonor on the regiment, as all other officers are allowed.

The pew I hold in the Episcopal Church at Alexandria shall be charged with an annual rent of five pounds, Virginia money; and I promise to pay an-

nually to the minister and vestry of the
Protestant Episcopal Church in Fairfax
Parish.

We are not graceless * at Mount Vernon.

June   1st,   Wednesday. — Went   to
Church and fasted all day.

BENEVOLENCE.

Having once or twice heard you speak
highly of the New Jersey College, as if
you had a desire of sending your son William there (who, I am told, is a youth
fond of study and instruction, and disposed to a studious life, in following which
he may not only promote his own happiness, but the future welfare of others), I
should be glad, if you have no other ob-
jection to it than the expense, if you would
send him to that college as soon as con-

---

* He always said grace at table.

venient, and depend on me for twenty-
five pounds a year for his support, so long
as it may be necessary for the completion
of his education.

If I live to see the accomplishment of
this term, the sum here stipulated shall
be annually paid. And if I die in the
meantime, this letter shall be obligation
upon my heirs·or executors to do it according to the true intent and meaning
hereof.

No other return is expected or wished
for this offer than that you accept it with
the same freedom and good-will with
which it is made, and that you may not
even consider it in the light of an obligation, or mention it as such; for be assured
that from me it will never be known.

ALEXANDRIA ACADEMY.

To the trustees . . . I give four thousand dollars; or, in other words, twenty of

the shares which I hold in the Bank of Alexandria, towards the support of *a free school*, established at, or annexed to, the Academy; for the purpose of educating such orphan children, or *the children of such other* poor *and indigent persons* as are unable to accomplish it with their own means, and who, in the judgment of the trustees of the seminary, are best entitled to the benefit of the donation.

When Washington was on his tour through New England in 1789, he visited Ipswich. Mr. Cleveland, the minister of the town, was presented to him. As he approached, hat in hand, Washington said: "Put on your hat, parson, and I will shake hands with you." "I can not wear my hat in your presence, General," said the parson, "when I think of what you have done for this country." "You did as

much as I." "No, no," protested the minister. "Yes," said Washington, "you did
what you could, and I have done no
more."

At the close of the Revolution, Washington received a letter from Colonel
Nicola, an intimate friend, containing the
proposition to make him king of America.
In reply to this letter, Washington wrote
these words: "With a mixture of great
surprise and astonishment, I have read
with attention the sentiments you have
submitted to my perusal. Be assured, sir,
no occurrence in the course of the war
has given me more painful sensations
than your information of there being such
ideas existing in the army as you have
expressed, and I must view with abhor-
rence and reprehend with severity. For
the present, the communication of them
will rest in my own bosom, unless some

further agitation of the matter shall make a disclosure necessary. I am much at a loss to conceive what part of my conduct could have given encouragement to an address which to me seems big with the greatest mischiefs that can befall my country. If I am not deceived in the knowledge of myself, you could not have found a person to whom your schemes are more disagreeable. At the same time, in justice to my own feelings, I must add, that no man possesses a more sincere wish to see ample justice done to the army than I do; and as far as my powers and influence, in a constitutional way, extend, they shall be employed to the utmost of my abilities to effect it, should there be any occasion. Let me conjure you, then, if you have any regard for your country, concern for yourself or posterity, or respect for me, to banish these thoughts from your mind, and never again communicate, or from yourself or any one else, a sentiment of like nature."

The Ideal Patriot had defeated King George III of England, and repudiated "King George I of America."

DUTY.

The man who wishes to steer clear of shelves and rocks must know where they lie.

To persevere in one's duty and be silent, is the best answer to calumny.

I am resolved that no misrepresentations, falsehoods, or calumny shall make me swerve from what I conceive to be the strict line of duty.

CONSOLATION.

In looking forward to that awful moment when I must bid adieu to sublunary things, I anticipate the consolation of

leaving our country in a prosperous condition. And while the curtain of separation shall be drawing, my last breath will,
I trust, expire in a prayer for the temporal
and eternal felicity of those who have not
only endeavored to gild the evening of
my days with unclouded serenity, but extended their desires to *my happiness here-
after* in a *brighter world.*

Do not flatter me with vain hopes. I
am not afraid to die, and therefore can
hear the worst.

Whether to-night or twenty years
hence makes no difference. I know that
I am in the hands of a good Providence.

CHAPTER XIV.

SAYINGS ABOUT WASHINGTON.

"FIRST in war, first in peace, and first in the hearts of his country-men."—*Henry Lee.*

"My fine crab-tree walking-stick with a gold head, and curiously wrought in the form of the Cap of Liberty, I give to my friend and the friend of mankind, George Washington. If it were a scepter he has merited it, and would become it."—*Benjamin Franklin (in his Will).*

"America has furnished to the world the character of a Washington. . . . If our American institutions had done nothing else, that alone would have entitled them to the respect of mankind."—*Daniel Webster.*

"The most illustrious and beloved personage which the country ever produced."—*John Adams.*

"Washington is the purest figure in
history. . . . If among all the pedestals
supplied by history for public characters ·
of extraordinary nobility and purity, I saw
one higher than all the rest, and if I were
required at a moment's notice to name
the fittest occupant for it, I think my
choice at any time during the last forty-
five years would have lighted, and it would
now light upon Washington."—*William
E. Gladstone.*

"His integrity was most pure."—
Thomas Jefferson.

"Next to the saints of religion must
be ranked in all our minds the saints of
our country. . . . Great, pure leaders, like
those of historic memory, enlarge polit-

ical philosophy into devotion. . . . The soldiers of Valley Forge saw in their general a lofty character, for whom they could endure privations, in whom they could trust. When they were cold and hungry and homesick, they were still inspired by the merit of their commander. He had separated himself from his wealth and its peace to be a soldier against the greatest power on earth; the troops saw that moral worth, and were cheered by the vision when all other scenes were darkened. When Baron Steuben, an ardent volunteer from the German army, saw the troops at Valley Forge, their want of all the comforts of life, he wondered what held the soldiers so firmly to their post of duty. It was a moral power that held them—the hope of a free nation and faith in their chieftain. In Philadelphia the British army, from the highest to the humblest, was spending in carousal the winter months, which the Colonial troops were spending in all forms of discomfort. One British officer kept a gambling-house, in which the common soldiers were robbed of their gold. Thus was the British army a military machine, while the American army was a band of men with a soul in it—an army of six thousand friends of freedom and of Washington. Washington's dining-room of logs, in which banqueting-hall, that could be duplicated for fifty dollars, there was simple food and no carousal, became an emblem of the kind of leader the file was trusting and following."—*David Swing.*

"Egad! he ran wonderfully! We had nobody, hereabouts, that could come near him. There was young Langhorne Dade, of Westmoreland, a confounded clean-made, tight young fellow, and a mighty swift runner, too; but he was no match for George."—*An Old Gentleman Neighbor.*

In 1785, John Hunter visited Mount Vernon, and describes a tour through Washington's stables: "Went to see his famous horse, Magnolia—a most beautiful creature. A whole length of his was taken awhile ago (mounted on Magnolia) by a famous man from Europe on copper. I afterwards went to his stables, where, among an amazing number of horses, I saw old Nelson, now twenty-two years of age, that carried the general almost always during the war. Blueskin, another fine old horse next to him, now and then had that honor. Shaw also showed me his old servant, that was reported to have been taken with a number of the general's papers about him. They have heard the roaring of many a cannon in their time. Blueskin was not the favorite, on account of his not standing fire so well as venerable old Nelson." A serious fault to a man like Washington.

"He was one of the few entirely good men, in whom goodness had no touch of weakness; one of the rigorously just, in whom justice was not commingled with any severity of personal temper."—*Rufus W. Griswold.*

"Every one who met Washington told of the commanding presence and noble person, the ineffable dignity, and the calm, simple, and stately manners. No man ever left Washington's presence without a feeling of reverence and respect amounting almost to awe. I will quote only a single one of the many descriptions of Washington, and I select it because,

although it is the least favorable of the
many I have seen, and is written in
homely phrase, it displays the most evident and entire sincerity. The extract is
from a letter written by David Ackerson,
of Alexandria, Va., in 1811, in answer to
an inquiry by his son. Mr. Ackerson
commanded a company in the Revolutionary War. 'Washington was not,' he
wrote, 'what ladies would call a pretty
man, but in military costume a heroic figure, such as would impress the memory
ever afterwards.'

"The writer had a good view of Washington three days before the crossing of
the Delaware. 'Washington,' he says,
'had a large, thick nose, and it was very
red that day, giving me the impression
that he was not so moderate in the use
of liquors as he was supposed to be. I
found afterwards that this was a peculiar-

ity. His nose was apt to turn scarlet in a cold wind. He was standing near a small camp-fire, evidently lost in thought and making no effort to keep warm. He seemed six feet and a half in height, was as erect as an Indian, and did not for a moment relax from a military attitude. Washington's exact height was six feet two inches in his boots. He was then a little lame from striking his knee against a tree. His eye was so gray that it looked almost white, and he had a troubled look on his colorless face. He had a piece of woolen tied around his throat, and was quite hoarse. Perhaps the throat trouble from which he finally died had its origin about then. Washington's boots were enormous. They were number 13. His ordinary walking shoes were number 11. His hands were large in proportion, and he could not buy a glove to fit him, and

had to have his gloves made to order.
His mouth was his strong feature, the lips
being always tightly compressed. That
day. they were compressed so tightly as
to be painful to look at. At that time he
weighed two hundred pounds, and there
was no surplus flesh about him. He was
tremendously muscled, and the fame of
his great strength was everywhere. His
large tent, when wrapped up with the
poles, was so heavy that it required two
men to place it in the camp-wagon.
Washington would lift it with one hand
and throw it in the wagon as easily as if it
were a pair of saddle-bags. He could hold
a musket with one hand, and shoot with
precision as easily as other men did with
a horse-pistol. His lungs were his weak
point, and his voice was never strong. He
was at that time in the prime of life. His
hair was a chestnut-brown, his cheeks

were prominent, and his head was not large in contrast to every other part of his body, which seemed large and bony at all points. His finger-joints and wrists were so large as to be genuine curiosities. . . . He was an enormous eater, but was content with bread and meat if he had plenty of it. . . . I saw him at Alexandria a year before he died. His hair was very gray, and his form was slightly bent.'

"This description is certainly not a flattering one, and all other accounts, as well as the best portraits, prove that Washington was a much handsomer man than this letter would indicate. Yet the writer, despite his freedom from all illusions and his readiness to state frankly all defects, was profoundly impressed by Washington's appearance as he watched him meditating by the camp-fire at the crisis of his country's fate, and herein lies the principal interest of his description."—*Henry Cabot Lodge.*

"This serene, inflexible, decisive man, biding his hour, could be then the venturesome soldier, willing to put every fortune on a chance, risking himself with a courage that alarmed men for his life. Does any but a fool think that he could have been all these things, and not have had in him the wild blood of passion? He had a love for fine clothes and show. He was, I fear, at times extravagant, and, as I have heard, could not pay his doctor's bill, and would postpone that, and send him a horse and a little money to educate his godson, the doctor's son. As to some of his letters, they contained jests not gross, but not quite fit for grave seigniors. . . . Was he religious? I do not know. Men say so. He might have been, and yet have his hours of ungoverned rage, or of other forms of human weakness.   Like a friend of mine, he was not given to speech concerning his creed. . . . He had no tricks of the demagogue.   He coveted no popularity.   He knew not to seek favor by going freely among men. . . . And yet this reserved aristocrat had to the end the love and confidence of every soldier in the ranks."—*S. Weir Mitchell.*

"General Washington is, I believe, almost the only man of an exalted character who does not lose some part of his respectability by intimate acquaintance.   I have never found a single thing that could lessen my respect for him.   A complete knowledge of his honesty, uprightness, and candor in all his private transactions, has sometimes led me to think him more than man."—*Mr. Lear (Washington's Sec-retary, a graduate of Harvard).*

"He never was known to tell a war story. Not that it is a sin to tell war stories; far from it. If the veteran sur-vivor of many a bloody encounter may not fight his battles o'er again, even in the ears of his friends, then is human na-ture brutal, and freedom a taunting lie. . . . But Washington never told a war story; no wonder that most pictures of him show him with a lower jaw that is 'set' as defiantly as if its owner were de-termined that nothing should escape him."—*John Habberton.*

"I have sometimes made him laugh most heartily from sympathy with my joy-ous and extravagant spirits." — *Miss Custis.*

18

"When, long ago, the ax-men went into the woods to find among the trees one suitable to be shaped into a mast for a large clipper ship, thousands of trees had to be passed by with only a glance. One tree had been twisted by the wind; one had been creased by the lightning; one had, when young, been bent down by some playing bears; one had been too near to its neighbors, and had been dwarfed in the top; one had been too near a stream, and had had too much sun and air on the side next the water, its trunk had bent towards its greatest limb; one had in youth been scorched by the fire of a hunter. At last a tree is found from which all defects are wanting, and up, straight as a draftsman's rule, runs the wooden shaft for a hundred feet. The woodsmen all rejoice, for the mast is found. The tree is elected from amid its fellows, and soon, instead of wearing its verdure in the forest, it goes careening on the ocean, holding up white sails to the journeying wind. Not otherwise when some weak Colonies need a chieftain for war and peace; they must pass by many a name great in fame before they find the citizen who holds all the virtues they know and love. No one dare say that Washington was the only man who could have performed the needed task. There may have been one other or many others who could have led the people to independence. The one man having been found, the people did not pursue longer the search. Such a search would be a foolish task for an historian. Having found the mast, the ax-men left the woods."—*David Swing.*

"He does what he thinks he ought to do. . . . Here is the finest instance in history of the success of moral power. . . . This is certain, that the eagerness of men to believe that pure, moral power carries empire with it, is the reason why men study with personal interest the life and character of Washington. His success seems to give a warrant for the triumph of humanity. In his success men believe that they will not for any long time be given over to the sway of men who are merely intellectual tricksters or giants of physical force. Men agree to honor Washington, because in his life they think they have a demonstration that right is might."—*Edward Everett Hale.*

"It is refreshing to find that he sometimes departed from the solemn, dull, conventional language of State papers, and calls the British soldiers 'Red Coats,' and General Putnam 'Old Put;' talks of 'kicking up some dust,' 'making a rumpus,' of nominating 'men not fit for shoe-blacks;' speaks of 'the rascally Puritanism of New England,' and 'the rascally Tories;' 'a scoundrel from Marblehead—a man of property.' But, in general, his style is plain and business-like, without fancy or figure of speech."—*Theodore Parker.*

"He had every title to command. Heaven, in giving him the higher qualities of the soul, had given also the tumultuous passions which accompany greatness and frequently tarnish its luster. With them was his first contest, and his first victory was over himself."—*Gouverneur Morris.*

"A conqueror for the *freedom* of his country; a legislator for its *security;* a magistrate for its *happiness*, with no selfish ambition or criminal thirst for power."—*London Courier.*

"He loved his country well enough to hold his success in serving it an ample recompense. But when his country needed sacrifices that no other man could or perhaps would make, he did not even hesitate. This was virtue in its most exalted character. . . .

"More than once he put his fame at hazard, when he had reason to think it would be sacrificed, at least in his age. Two instances can not be denied: First, when the army was disbanded; and, second, when he stood, like Leonidas at the Pass of Thermopylæ, to defend our independence against France. . . .

"The unambitious life of Washington, declining fame, yet courted by it, seemed like his own Potomac, widening and deep-

ening his channel as he approached the
sea, and displaying the usefulness and serenity of his greatness towards the end of
his course."—*Fisher Ames.*

"He did the two greatest things which,
in politics, man can have the privilege of
attempting. He maintained, by peace,
that independence of his country which
he had acquired by war. He founded a
free Government in the name of the principles of order, and by re-establishing
their sway; both tasks were accomplished
when he retired from public life."—*Guizot.*

"England has some share in his glory.
Although she can not number him among
those who have extended her provinces
or augmented her dominions, she may
at least feel a legitimate pride in the vic-
tories he achieved, in the great qualities
he exhibited in the contest with herself,

and indulge with satisfaction in the reflection that the vast empire which neither the ambition of Louis XIV nor the power of Napoleon could dismember, received its first shock from the courage which she had communicated to her own offspring, and that real liberty has arisen in that nation alone which inherited in its veins the genuine principle of British freedom."— *Archibald Alison.*

"Never in the tide of time has any man lived who had in so great a degree the almost divine faculty to command the confidence of his fellow-men, and rule the willing. Wherever he became known— in his family, in his neighborhood, his county, his native State, the continent, the camp, the civil life, the United States, among common people, in foreign courts throughout the civilized world of the human race, and even among savages—he, beyond all other men, had the confidence of his kind."—*George Bancroft.*

"It will be the duty of the historian and the sage in all ages to omit no occasion of commemorating this illustrious man, and until time shall be no more will a test of the progress which our race has made in wisdom and virtue be derived from the veneration paid to the immortal name of Washington."—*Lord Brougham.*

Providence left him childless, that his country might call him father."—*H. T. Tuckerman.*

"To the appointment of Washington, far more than to any other single circumstance, is due the ultimate success of the American Revolution, though in purely intellectual powers Washington was certainly inferior to Franklin and perhaps to two or three other of his colleagues."— *William E. H. Lecky.*

"What manner of people ought we to be in return for this great gift? We may bring forth others like him. There is more hope, not less of another Washington, from having had the first. We say of a great genius like Shakespeare or Raphael, that he is inimitable. But Washington was not a genius in the ordinary acceptation of that term. His perfections are imitable, on an humbler scale. Personal integrity, indefatigable industry, deferring self to duty, true brotherhood towards mankind, and a sincere desire to co-operate with God in doing good, may make many a Washington of whom the world may never hear." — *Caroline M. Kirkland.*

"George Washington will always receive the love and reverence of men, because they see embodied in him the noblest possibilities of humanity." — *Henry Cabot Lodge.*

"Washington served us chiefly by his sublime moral qualities. To him belonged the proud distinction of being the leader of a revolution, without awakening one doubt or solicitude as to the spotless purity of his purpose. His was the glory of being the brightest manifestation of the spirit which reigned in this country; and in this way he became a source of energy, a bond of union, the center of an enlightened people's confidence."—*William E. Channing.*

"From 1749 till 1784, and from 1789 till 1797, or a period of forty years, Washington filled offices of one kind or another,

and when he died he still held a commission. Thus, excluding his boyhood, there
were but seven years of his life in which
he was not engaged in public service.
Even after his retirement from the Presi-
dency, he served on a grand jury, and
before this he had several times acted as
petit juror. In another way he was a good
citizen, for when at Mount Vernon he invariably attended the election, rain or
shine, though it was a ride of ten miles
to the polling town."—*Paul Leicester
Ford.*

"He rode upon his farms entirely un-
attended. Mr. Custis, his adopted son,
gave this direction to a gentleman who
was out in search of Washington: 'You
will meet, sir, with an old gentleman riding alone, in plain, drab clothes, a broad-
brimmed, white hat, a hickory switch in

his hand, and carrying an umbrella with a long staff, which is attached to his saddle-bow—that person, sir, is General Washington.'

"So carefully did Washington manage his farms, that they became very productive. So noted were these products for their quality, and so faithfully were they put up, that any barrel of flour bearing the brand, 'GEO. WASHINGTON, MOUNT VERNON,' was exempted from customary inspection in British West India ports."

Erskine, so chary of his praise, so slow of faith in his fellows, inscribed in a set of his works as a present to Washington: "You, sir, are the only individual for whom I ever felt an awful reverence."

"He was a sincere believer in the Christian faith."—*Chief-Justice Marshall.*

"A Christian in faith and practice."— *Jared Sparks.*

"I am not surprised at what George has done. He was always a good boy."— *Washington's Mother.*

"This is the one hundred and tenth anniversary of the birthday of Washington. We are met to celebrate this day. Washington is the mightiest name of earth— long since mightiest in the cause of civil liberty, still mightiest in moral reformation. On that name a eulogy is expected. It can not be. To add brightness to the sun or glory to the name of Washington is alike impossible. Let none attempt it. In solemn awe pronounce the name, and let its naked, deathless splendor leave it shining on."—*Abraham Lincoln.*

www.ingramcontent.com/pod-product-compliance
Lightning Source LLC
Chambersburg PA
CBHW030621030726
47497CB00006B/1582